9/06

DO-OVER

christine
hurley
deriso

delacorte press

Published by
Delacorte Press
an imprint of
Random House Children's Books
a division of Random House, Inc.
New York

Text copyright © 2006 by Christine Hurley Deriso

Jacket illustration copyright © 2006 by Michelle Grant

Visit us on the Web! www.randomhouse.com/teens
Educators and librarians, for a variety of teaching tools, visit us at
www.randomhouse.com/teachers

Library of Congress Cataloging-in-Publication Data
Deriso, Christine Hurley.
Do-over / Christine Hurley Deriso.
p. cm.
Summary: Seventh-grader Elsa moves to a new town and starts a new
school where, with the help of her recently deceased mother and a magic
locket that allows her to redo the last ten seconds in any situation,
she attempts to become popular.
ISBN 0-385-73333-X (trade) — ISBN 0-385-90350-2 (glb)
[1. Conduct of life—Fiction. 2. Popularity—Fiction. 3. Magic—Fiction.
4. Middle schools—Fiction. 5. Moving, Household—Fiction.
6. Grief—Fiction. 7. Schools.] I. Title.
PZ7.D4427Do 2006
[Fic]—dc22   2005013199

The text of this book is set in 12-point Goudy.

Book design by Kenny Holcomb

Printed in the United States of America

June 2006

10 9 8 7 6 5 4 3 2 1

To my parents, Gregory and Jane Hurley, who taught me to love writing, and to my amazing children, who give me so much to write about. And to my husband, Graham . . . always.

ONE

"You're kidding."

Why do people say that only when there's not a single chance, not one in a zillion, that what they've just heard is a joke?

Still, that's what I said when my dad told me we were moving.

"You're kidding."

It's the same thing I said one day almost a year earlier, after walking home from school. The air was honeysuckle-scented, the grass was damp from a morning shower and my arms were swinging in the breeze. No backpack. It was a Friday, I'd just celebrated my twelfth birthday four days earlier and sixth grade would be over in a week. Everything was perfect.

Except it wasn't. I found out that day that sometimes perfect is perfectly horrible but you don't know it yet.

Clue number one was the police car in my driveway. That was a first. The car was empty, but the engine was running and the flashing light was on, spinning around like a retro disco ball.

That was the car I noticed first. But other cars were in the driveway, too, and still others were parked along the curb. I was dumb enough to feel a little twinge of excitement, like I was walking into a surprise party or something. But I'd never had a surprise party, and why would a police officer be invited, and what was the occasion anyhow, and . . . weird ideas like these were bouncing randomly around in my head when . . .

When my life fell apart.

Dad had spotted me through the window and he came running out of the house. He had been on the track team in high school and was still a really fast runner. He was barreling at me so fast, I thought he'd knock me to the ground. But the instant he reached me, he wrapped his arms around me and sobbed into my ear. My dad sobbing . . . This was a first, too. I was beginning to hate firsts.

I don't remember his words, or how many people crowded around us, or whether I noticed that my blouse was wet with Dad's tears, or the instant when I knew that all I wanted in the whole wide world was to see my mom, who was nowhere in sight, because . . .

She was dead.

"You're kidding," I said.

Except I knew he wasn't.

Tough break for a twelve-year-old, right? Isn't a twelve-year-old supposed to worry about fractions and training bras?

Who changed the rules of my life? And why wasn't I consulted?

But that's what happened. My mom was dead of some weird brain problem I'd never heard of and couldn't even spell (*a-n-e-u-r-y-s-m*, I learned after checking a dictionary). I didn't even have a chance to say goodbye. The whole world caved in, and only ten seconds before, everything had been perfect, and . . .

I wanted a do-over.

TWO

"You're kidding!"

Now it was Lani's turn to say it. Note the exclamation point. If Lani's name was in the dictionary, it would be followed by an exclamation point. She was my best friend, but I have to admit that she was heavy on emoting. Mom used to call her Triple-L: Larger-than-Life Lani.

"I'm not kidding," I said glumly, unfolding sleeping bags beside my bed for our weekly Friday-night sleepover. "I really am moving."

Dad had told me the night before, so I was still absorbing the news myself. Lani clutched her chest in her best drama queen impersonation. "Omigod, Elsa! You said you had big news, but I didn't know your big news would ruin my life! Moving!" She moaned. *"When?"*

"Next weekend, just before the start of spring semester."

"N-next w-weekend . . . ," Lani repeated, sputtering the words. *"Where?"*

"Harbin Springs, just sixty miles from here." I shrugged, trying to sound like it was no big deal. I felt terrible, but Lani was dramatic enough for both of us. "No big change." One South Carolina town was pretty much like another . . . stubby little palmetto trees lining every main street, dainty pink azaleas and fuchsia crepe myrtle on every lawn and enough humidity in the summer to choke a horse, but lots of crisp, shimmery days in the other seasons, including occasional afternoons in the dead of winter so warm you could go outside barefoot.

"Why are you moving, Elsa?" Lani wailed, working her way through a reporter's list of who-what-where-when-why. My stomach hurt. I hoped she was running out of *W*s.

"My dad got a new job. It's a smaller bank, but he'll have some big-shot title that he's really psyched about." I managed a sad smile and tugged at Lani's thick auburn hair. "He told me he could commute until summer starts so I could finish seventh grade here, but I figure now is as good a time as any to take the leap."

"You're insane!" Lani shrieked.

I smiled. "It's not so bad," I insisted. "Harbin Springs is close to the ocean. Dad said you can visit anytime and he'll take us to Myrtle Beach. Plus, we'll live with Grandma, at least until we find our own place. Dad says the fresh start will do us good."

"A fresh start? In the middle of seventh grade?" Lani jumped to her feet, flinging her hands in the air. "We don't make fresh starts without each other! How will I survive the Slice Girls without you?"

The Slice Girls' real names were Rebecca, Blaise and Selena, but since the start of middle school, they'd been the Slice Girls to us. It was our secret joke, based on how they cut their eyes at us to let us know they were now way out of our league, popularity-wise. "The look" surgically removed our self-esteem, dunked it in formaldehyde and left it in the science lab as an official "Geeks as Life-Form" specimen. It made no sense, really; it hadn't been long at all since we were all doing cartwheels together in each other's front yards and selling lemonade from the curb. But middle school started and Snob City.

I felt a little pinch in my heart. It wasn't any fun being unpopular, but, well, with Lani, it actually kinda *was*. We were unpopular *together*. It was Lani who defended me when the Slice Girls made fun of my freckles, telling them with a sneer that they were beauty marks. It was Lani who puffed out her chest and told them that we made our *own* fashion rules when they laughed at me for wearing babyish corduroy overalls (and high-waters at that!) on the first day of school. Lani even wore *her* overalls the next day for solidarity. It was Lani who made me feel good about my limp light brown hair (versatile, she called it) and my long skinny legs (a model's legs, once my scabby knees healed up, she assured me).

Lani was a great friend. I jumped to my feet and gave her a hug. "I'll miss you," I said. "But don't worry about the Slice Girls. You can take care of yourself. And you can visit me as often as you want. Every weekend, practically."

"It won't be the same!" Lani said.

I plopped backward onto my bed. "I don't know . . . maybe it's not such a bad thing." I gazed up at the ceiling. "You know, before my mom died last year, I was just Elsa. Not too tall, not too short, not too skinny, not too fat, not too smart, not too dumb, not too pretty, not too hideous . . . just Elsa."

"What are you talking about?" Lani said. "You're still just Elsa."

"No. Now, to everybody except the Slice Girls, who would hate me with or without a mother, I'm Poor Elsa. Poor-Elsa-whose-mother-died. Maybe at a new school, I can be just Elsa again."

"Nobody treats you differently," Lani said, but her heart wasn't in it. Actually, though I would never say so, Lani's own mom was Exhibit A.

Mrs. Evans had always been nice to me, but before Mom died, she was nice in a brisk, "hi-Elsa-now-you-girls-get-out-from-under-my-feet" kind of way. After Mom died, she became nice to me in a gaze-in-my-eyes-and-ask-me-if-I'm-REEEALLY-okay kind of way. It was sweet, but our conversations never felt natural anymore.

"Hiiii, Elsa," Mrs. Evans would say, drawing out her vowels in a way I'd never heard her do before. "Ya okaaay, honey? You reeaally okay? Ya shooo-er?"

Kinda creeped me out. I hadn't only lost my mom. I had lost my averageness. I wanted it back.

Lani and I were on the same wavelength about almost everything, but this I didn't think she could understand.

She plopped down on the bed beside me. We were quiet for a minute, staring at the glow-in-the-dark plastic stars on my ceiling. "What's it like to lose your mom?" Lani asked quietly.

I paused. Lani had spent the past year making sure we talked about anything *other* than my mom, as if avoiding the subject could keep me from thinking about her. I wasn't prepared for a head-on question. Besides, how do you answer a question like that? I thought for a minute.

"I wish I'd made a list of questions to ask her before she died," I said softly. "You know . . . things only a mom can answer, like how you keep from poking yourself in the eye when you put that gloppy black stuff on your lashes. And why you put that gloppy black stuff on your lashes in the first place.

"And how you unbunch your underpants so that nobody will notice," I continued, feeling silly and sad at the same time.

"Well, I can tell you that," Lani said, trying to sound helpful.

There was more, too, though. I guess I didn't realize I had so many questions until I didn't have a mom to ask anymore.

Finally, I said, "Think of everything it means to have a mom, then subtract it all." I laced my fingers together and laid my hands on my chest. "That's what it's like."

"You still have your dad," Lani said. "He can help you."

"Yeah, and he's awesome. But . . ." I propped myself up on an elbow. "Take the Slice Girls, for instance. If they dissed us at school and I told my dad, he'd say, 'Oh, honey, that's just how kids are at your age. Don't let it bother you.'" Lani laughed at my deep, throaty Dad imitation. "But if I told my *mom*, she'd have a look in her eye that let me know she was feeling the exact same thing I was feeling. I miss that look."

I sighed. Funny thing about those stars on my ceiling . . . In the dark, they glowed, but in daylight, they just blended into the background. Dusk was just starting to settle outside, so I had to squint hard to see their outlines.

Yup. Still there.

✪

"It's gonna be fine, you know."

Dad squeezed my hand as we sprawled lazily together in our backyard hammock. Lani had gone home, and he joined me in the hammock as the lazy stillness of a Saturday evening settled in.

"Moving to a new place isn't the end of the world," he said softly. "Harbin Springs is a nice little town, and the middle school has a great reputation. It's the same school your mom went to, and look how brilliant she turned out to be."

I smiled. Dad and I didn't talk about Mom much, but we didn't avoid talking about her. I think we each just knew how the other felt.

"Are you sure you don't want to finish the school year here?" he asked gently.

"Things just feel a little weird here, you know? Besides, I'm looking forward to being with Grandma. I could use a woman's touch, don't you think, dahling?" I joked in my best diva accent.

"What am I, chopped liver?" Dad asked, pinching me playfully. "I can even give you my makeup tips, if you ask really nicely."

I laughed. Dad always made me laugh.

"Sure, you're the makeup expert in the family," I teased, "but who will help me with my essays?" That had always been Mom's job. She was a writer, doing funny little essays for the local magazine and starting novels she was sure she could publish, if only she ever finished one.

"Hey, give me a chance!" Dad said. "I won a contest in fourth grade for writing about my hero."

I grinned. "Who was your hero?"

"Genevieve Lawler, of course, the most efficient school librarian ever. True, she had the personality of an eggplant, but that gal knew the Dewey decimal system like the back of her hand. Ya gotta admire that in a person."

I rolled my eyes. "Let me guess: She judged the essay contest, right?"

"A sheer coincidence."

I giggled and Dad squeezed me closer. "We're gonna be fine, Elsa," he said softly.

I burrowed my head into his chest. My mom was gone, my best friend would soon live sixty miles away from me and I was about to endure the most daunting of all challenges: starting a new school toward the end of seventh grade. But with a dad as cool as mine, how bad could things be?

THREE

Dad and I didn't talk much as we drove to Harbin Springs with a U-Haul full of furniture cruising behind us. I had packed my whole life into that trailer: scrapbooks, CDs, dolphin posters, goofy pictures with Lani and me sticking out our tongues in an amusement park booth.

The window was open and my hair flew in the breeze. Dad had turned on the radio a couple of times, but nothing seemed to suit him, and now it was quiet. Quiet except for the rustle of the breeze as we left our old life in the dust.

Are you there, Mom? I asked in my mind. I did that a lot lately. Don't worry; I wasn't going mental. I just liked talking to her in my head, even if she couldn't answer. I pretended she could. At least I *think* I was pretending. Sometimes, it seemed like she was actually there.

Mom, this really sucks, I said in my head as Dad cruised

along the interstate. *Here I am, moving to a new town. And no matter where I go, you're not there, which, by the way, is, like, so unfair. Moms aren't supposed to die before their kids are grown, are they? I think there's some kinda rule. . . .*

My eyes stayed focused on the road without seeing anything at all.

I'm mad at you, Mom, I continued in my head. *That's nuts, huh? Mad at you for dying . . . But I can't help it. In fact, I'm more than mad. I'm furious. At you. At you, Mom. Do you hear me, Mom? How dare you die on me?*

I blinked quickly to push back the tears forming in my eyes. My stare returned to the blur of asphalt.

But more than anything, I just miss you.

Dad turned off an exit I knew like the back of my hand. We'd visited Grandma's house a lot over the years. Off the exit was a soft-drink bottling plant that signaled that Grandma's house was another quarter of a mile. In two minutes, we arrived in Grandma's neighborhood, full of neat little ranch-style brick houses with flower beds and window boxes. Most of her neighbors were retired, so there was a sleepy but comforting feel to the tidy, tree-lined streets. These same retirees were raising their families when Mom grew up here, and she said that in those days the neighborhood was always full of kids on bikes and skates. There were front-yard games of kickball, and games of hide-and-seek that wound from one yard to the next as teams got more creative with their hiding places. Mom told me how much fun it was to be one of a dozen sweaty, mosquito-bitten kids who played in the summer from morning until dusk, when parents started gathering on front porches to call them home for dinner.

Now everything was quiet. The kids were all grown, and the folks left behind spent their time trimming hedges and pulling weeds. Before Mom died, coming here felt as safe and comfy as my ratty old bathrobe. Now it seemed . . . different. The kind of different that makes your stomach hurt.

As we drove up the street, a couple of Grandma's neighbors waved at us. We waved back. Mrs. Willis, Mrs. Mulligan . . . we knew them all by name.

Dad pulled into Grandma's driveway and tooted the horn twice—short toot followed by long toot. *Dut-dooooo.* That was his official driveway greeting. The front door opened and Grandma was smiling, waving us inside.

"Come in, come in!" she sang, her hand fluttering like a little bird. She hugged me as I stepped onto her front porch.

"There's my girl," she said. "I've got the house all ready for you. You'll sleep in your regular spot, of course . . . your mom's old room!"

She smiled brightly as she said it, but her blue eyes suddenly sparkled with tears. I squeezed her hands.

"It's okay, Grandma," I whispered.

She swallowed hard. "Okay? It's *better* than okay! I have my darling Elsa all to myself! And guess what, I've got a five-thousand-piece puzzle already started for us in the den. We're gonna have so much fun!"

I smiled. "Careful, now, Grandma. You wouldn't want to trigger my heart condition with all this excitement."

She looked startled. "Heart condition . . . !" Then she

started laughing. "Oh, Elsa. Just like your mom, with your dry sense of humor."

Dad joined us on the porch, lugging a suitcase in each hand.

"Hi, Jack," Grandma said, pecking him on the cheek. "Let's get you two settled."

I bounded up the stairs to Mom's old room. It hadn't been redecorated since she was a kid, so it was kind of like a Mom Museum, all pink and white dotted swiss. Her old Holly Hobby doll leaned stiffly against the pillow on the bed, smiling with faded red lips. As I walked around the room and envisioned where I'd hang my dolphin posters and set up my computer, I touched Mom's pretty face peering out of pictures on the dresser. Mom and her girlfriends at the beach. Mom snuggling with her cat on the sofa. Mom at her high school graduation, with Grandma and Grandpa beaming proudly by her side. And on the bedside table, a photo of Mom and me, with Mom squeezing me from behind and both of us laughing. Both with shoulder-length light brown hair. Both with a dusting of freckles on our noses. (Beauty marks, Lani would say.)

I smiled a little as my eyes wandered over to the bookshelf, decorated with Mom's collection of plaques, awards and ribbons. Swim team, essay contest, debate club, yearbook staff, high school newspaper. If the Mom Museum had a tour guide, I could hear his spiel now: "Ladies and gentlemen, you are witnessing the archives of a happy, normal kid. Elsa Alden's mother was pretty, popular, smart and outgoing. Historians can only guess why her daughter's destiny was to become a tragic, unpopular geek."

Okay, Mr. Tour Guide. You can shut up now.

Still, it was a bittersweet feeling to be exactly where my mom had been when she was my age. I unzipped a tote bag, retrieved my plastic stars, stood on my tiptoes on the bed and carefully stuck them to the ceiling. *There,* I thought. *Now this room will feel like home.*

I stepped off the mattress and walked over to the dresser. Grandma had emptied the drawers for me, but the top was still cluttered with little knickknacks. Some were left over from Mom's childhood, and others I had added to the collection over the years. I fingered them carefully, then noticed that something had slipped off and fallen on the floor. I bent over to pick it up. It was a gold necklace with a round locket, about the size of a quarter.

That's weird . . . , I thought. In all my visits, I'd never noticed it before, and I hadn't seen it lying there when I walked over to the dresser just then.

I peered at the locket, then wiped the smudges off with the bottom of my shirt and held it closer. Nothing special . . . just a gold locket (fake gold, probably) with a heart etched in the middle.

I let the necklace slide from my hand onto the dresser, thinking maybe I'd ask Grandma about it later.

✿

"How do I look?"

Why do people ask that question when the only answer they expect is "fine"?

But I asked it anyway as I walked into Grandma's

kitchen the next morning. My first day at Harbin Springs Middle School would begin in exactly—I checked my watch—twenty-seven minutes.

"You look beautiful, sweetie," Grandma said, kissing my cheek.

"Thanks, Grandma, but I'm not going for 'beautiful,' " I said with a smile. "I'm going for 'fine.' I just want to blend in today." I tucked my white shirt into my jeans.

"Mission accomplished," said Dad as he took a bite of toast at the table. "I didn't even know you were standing there. I thought you were part of the wallpaper."

"Funny." I kissed his cheek and ruffled his hair. "There. Now you'll blend in with everybody having a bad hair day."

"I thought I did that every day," he said.

Grandma smiled. "You're going to have a great day, honey," she said. "Just keep a smile on your face and everything will be fine."

Obviously, Grandma was a little naïve. But I wanted to believe her. Haven't we all known since preschool that others will treat us the way we treat them? I'm friendly, they're friendly. Right? That was my philosophy as I headed out to walk the four blocks to school. Yeah, I know what you're thinking. And you're right. I was delusional.

Oh, the day started out okay. The first ten minutes or so were actually bearable. As I walked toward the school, I could have sworn that a couple of people waved at me. Either that or they were swatting flies. Whatever. I waved back.

Once I reached the school, my first stop was the office. A

couple of ladies sat at desks behind a counter, but no one looked up, even after I cleared my throat a couple of times. *Smile*, I reminded myself nervously. *Smile*.

"Hi!" I said in a voice that I had commanded to sound friendly and confident but that came out all squeaky and petrified.

One of the ladies looked up. No smile.

"Uh . . . I'm Elsa Alden, and this is my first day. My dad registered me last week."

Grouchy Office Lady studied me blandly for a second or two, then started riffling through a folder on her desk, peering down through glasses that sat on the edge of her nose.

"Mmm-hmmmm," Grouchy Office Lady said. "Elsa Alden."

"Ah! So I really do exist!"

Dead silence.

Idiot, I muttered under my breath. *I'm an idiot.* In case you haven't noticed yet, I make really awful jokes when I'm nervous.

Grouchy Office Lady walked toward me, looking annoyed, and handed me a card over the counter. "Here's your schedule," she said. "Right now, report to Mr. Wright's class for homeroom and language arts."

"Mr. Wright, huh?" I said. "I guess I can't go wrong with him."

Dead silence.

Shut up, Elsa! Quit making lame remarks and just blend in!

The heavy office door creaked as a guy walked in. He was skinny with thick dark hair that fell into his eyes.

"Hi, Mrs. Stiffle," he said to Grouchy Office Lady. "Mr. Wright asked me to bring you these permission forms for Wednesday's field trip."

"Thank you, Martin," she said, taking the forms. "As long as you're here, will you walk this new girl back to class with you? You have all the same classes, so you can show her around today."

He looked hesitant as I managed a weak little smile. "I'm Elsa," I said.

"Martin King," he replied, looking at my shoes rather than my face. "No Luther in the middle. Just Martin King." He opened the door and held out his arm. "Right this way."

I tried to break the ice as we headed down the hall.

"Sorry you got stuck escorting me around," I said.

Martin smiled shyly, still apparently fascinated by the floor, because that was the only place he ever seemed to look. "You might be the sorry one. Hanging around with me seems to have a kamikaze effect on people."

"Kamikaze?"

He nodded. "Social suicide. Don't say I didn't warn you."

I wrinkled my brow. "I don't get it. Why is that?"

He shrugged absently. "I read J. D. Salinger during break period while everybody else passes around *Teen People*," he said. "Throw glasses and braces into the mix and you've got the complete geek package."

I smiled. "It's okay. I like books, too. My mom was a writer."

"Was?"

Stupid! Stupid! Stupid! Here I was, finally getting the chance to shed my stigma as the girl with the dead mom, and what do I do? I spill the beans before first period even begins. I felt my face flush.

"Yeah . . . ," I said, then quickly changed the subject. "J. D. Salinger. I haven't heard of that book. What's it about?"

Martin's lips tightened into a tiny smile. "J. D. Salinger isn't a book. He's a writer. He writes a lot about fitting in . . . well, about *not* fitting in, actually. I'll loan you my books if you're interested. Just remember: the kamikaze effect."

I smiled as we walked into Mr. Wright's classroom. "Consider me warned. And thanks for walking me to class."

The teacher looked up from his desk. "Ah. Elsa Alden?"

Blend in. Blend in. "Yes," I said quietly.

"Welcome to our class, where the wonders of great literature await."

I smiled nervously. "Sounds . . . wonderful."

A couple of the kids in the class rolled their eyes and groaned. *Stupid, stupid, stupid!* What in the world was happening to my plan to blend in? I was imploding before everyone's eyes.

Mr. Wright peered around the room. "Hmmm . . . Elsa, why don't you sit in the empty seat right behind Darcy."

He motioned toward a pretty girl with almond-shaped eyes and waist-length honey-colored hair accented by expertly applied blond highlights. The girl crinkled her nose.

"Not here, Mr. Wright!" she said with a pout, then flashed me a smile as fake as her highlights. "No offense," she explained. "It's just that I need to keep that seat empty for my gym bag. You know . . . cheerleading, dance class . . . all my stuff." Her lip curled. "Why don't you sit next to Martin? Looks like you two are already friends. . . ."

Snickers rippled through the classroom.

Mr. Wright raised an eyebrow. "Looks like your gym bag will have to find a new home, Darcy. Shove it. Your gym bag, that is. Under your desk." The class giggled and Darcy rolled her eyes. Mr. Wright turned back to me. "Miss Alden, have a seat, please."

As I walked toward my seat, Darcy's fake smile turned to a sneer. She snatched her gym bag out of my chair and flung her highlighted hair in my general direction.

Mr. Wright gathered some papers and handed a stack to the first person in every row. "Take one and pass them back," he instructed. When the stack reached Darcy's perfectly manicured hands, she flung it backward without bothering to turn around. The papers flew, and I was on my hands and knees scooping them up.

"Oops," Darcy said, shooting me an icy glare.

"These sheets," Mr. Wright said as I settled myself at my desk, "are rules for an essay contest."

My skin tingled. I loved essay contests.

"The topic," Mr. Wright continued, "is 'What I've Learned in Seventh Grade.' "

I groaned out loud.

"Elsa?" Mr. Wright said. Uh-oh. *Shut up, shut up!*

"Yes, sir?" I said in barely a whisper.

"Why the groan?" he asked, but his tone was friendly.

I shrugged. "Well, I really like to write," I said, "but it seems like essay contest topics are always so lame."

He smiled knowingly. "What *do* you like to write about?"

I brightened at the question. My mom and I used to spend countless hours at the computer, brainstorming a plot for a novel, then taking turns writing paragraphs. It was just for fun; Mom had been strictly business when she had a real writing assignment, but we loved the goofiness of feeding off each other's imagination and having to follow the nutty plot twists we created for each other.

"It's not that I like writing about anything specific," I answered carefully. "I just love noticing something that's right there in plain sight that nobody else has noticed . . . or thinking about something in a way that nobody else has thought about before. Then I write about it."

Darcy turned her head slightly toward me and cooed sarcastically, "*Oooohhh*. Fascinating."

I blushed. Why couldn't I just keep my big mouth shut?

But Mr. Wright looked pleased. "I'm looking forward to reading your work," he told me. "And why don't we start with this essay? What could be more challenging than taking some tired, trite subject and making it fresh?" He gestured to the class. "That goes for all of you. The essay contest is optional, but you'll get extra credit if you write one, and it'll be great practice. The essays are due May fifth, and the winner will read his or her essay in the auditorium for the whole school on Honors Day, May ninth. And I left out one small detail." He grinned and paused for dramatic effect. "The *Harbin Springs Tribune* is donating a new laptop computer to the winner."

The classroom tingled with a sudden infusion of energy.

"Oh, Mr. Wright!" Darcy gushed, raising her hand high.

"I have lots to write about! Cheerleading and dancing and . . ."

"Right, Darcy," he said slowly. "But I think Elsa's on the right track. You should move beyond the obvious and find a way to share something really meaningful with the reader."

Darcy huffed. "Well, I have *lots* of meaningful things to say," she said. She shot me another icy glare. "We'll see who wins that laptop."

I sank deeper into my chair. Here it was the first day of school, and I was managing to annoy the girl who probably had her picture pasted next to the word "popular" in the dictionary. I was blending in . . . but the way strawberries do when you toss them into a blender with milk and ice cream. Blending in—in a shredded, pummeled and pulverized kind of way.

✿

I managed to keep a low profile for the next couple of hours. I quickly figured out that my best course of action was not to talk, move or breathe, if possible. But making like a statue can attract pigeons, if you know what I mean, and soon enough, the pigeons came calling.

"Why so quiet?" Darcy asked as we settled into our fourth-period class.

I shrugged. "Not much to say."

She turned to a friend and giggled. "Oooh, Jade, she's giving us the silent treatment."

Jade, with shiny black hair and sparkly eyes, giggled

back. She was prettier than Darcy, but Darcy was clearly the leader.

"Oh, *please* talk to us, Elsie," Darcy said.

"It's Elsa," I corrected.

"Can't I give you a little nickname? I like Elsie. Isn't that the name of the cow on the milk carton?"

I looked up at her from my notebook. "My name is Elsa."

"Elsa, Elsie . . . what's the diff? Anyhow, El*sahhhh,* Jade and I were wondering if you wanted to sit with us at lunch next period."

You know that bright red WARNING sign that flashes on spaceship modules in movies right before the explosion? That's the sign that was flashing in my head. How was I supposed to respond to Darcy's lunch invitation? If I said yes, I was setting myself up for more Elsie the Cow–type remarks, or worse. On the other hand, if I said no, she would label me a snob, at which point the claws would *really* come out, and I'd be sitting all by myself at lunch, perfectly defenseless as she and her friends whispered and giggled, tossing too-cool glances my way. This was a no-win situation, and omigod, it was only my first day of school.

"Sure. I'll sit with you at lunch." There. I said it. "Thanks for asking."

I was on my way to the lionesses' den. So much for blending in.

✿

I smiled at the cafeteria lady filling my plate with mystery meat, then followed Darcy to a table where her clique sat waiting for their Leader. They parted, clearing the throne for Queen Darcy. She sat in the empty chair, then shot a glance at me.

"Oh," she said. "*She's* sitting with us, too." A clique member jumped up and fetched me a seat, placing it just outside their circle.

I tried to smile. "Hi, everybody," I said in my squeaky-petrified voice.

The girls looked at Darcy. She smiled demurely, which was the permission they needed to turn to me and say hi.

Darcy sounded bored as she made brisk introductions. "Everybody, this is Elsie . . . oh, I mean *Elsaaaahhh*," she cooed. "Elsa, you met Jade last period," she said, pointing to the brunette, "and this is Carter and Jen."

"Hi," I said, smiling shyly.

"So, Elsa," Darcy said, "tell us about yourself."

I shrugged. "Not much to tell. I like sports. I like dolphins. Dolphins are kinda my thing."

Darcy curled a lip. "Your thing? O-*kay*. . . ."

"Dolphins?" Carter piped up. "You mean like Shampoo?"

My eyebrows knitted together. *Shampoo* . . . "Oh, you must mean Shamu," I said. "He's a whale."

Darcy twirled a finger in the air. "What*ever*," she said, then muttered under her breath, "Very mature."

The girls snickered, and I slid lower in my seat.

"Hey, Elsa," Darcy continued, casting a quick sideways glance at Jade. "Wanna come to a sleepover this Friday night? Jade, Jen and Carter are coming. It'll be *sweet*."

A sleepover? Just like the old days with Lani! My mood

lightened for a moment. "A sleepover?" I asked hesitantly. "Really?"

"Of course, silly!" Darcy cooed. "It'll be totally awesome."

"Well . . ." *Stop being so uptight, Elsa,* I told myself impatiently. *Just say yes!* "Sure. I'd love to."

My words hung in the air for a second before the girls exploded into giggles, making sputtering noises through their lips.

"I'm, like, totally kidding!" Darcy finally said, dropping her jaw to indicate how amazed she was by my stupidity. "No offense, Elsa. I just thought for sure you'd know that sleepovers are, like, *so* sixth grade."

I felt like a fan was blowing hot air directly onto my face. I gazed down at my lunch tray, clueless about how to respond.

"But hey, Elsa," Jade chirped, "if you really think it would be super-awesome to have a sleepover of your own, my little sister has a pair of footie pajamas that you can borrow."

The girls giggled some more and slapped high fives.

I stabbed a bite of mystery meat with my fork and gulped it down, just to have something to do. No way was I hungry.

"So," Darcy said after they'd settled down, "I heard you hooked up with Martin. He's, like, the star of the school baseball team, you know. Mr. Hand-Eye Coordination, that's what everybody calls him."

The other girls stuffed giggles into the backs of their throats.

I was confused. "What?"

Darcy nodded toward a table where Martin sat alone, his head buried in a book. "Martin," she repeated. "I heard he's your boyfriend."

WARNING. WARNING. WARNING. "We just met this morning. I don't even know him," I said.

"Oh, so you *don't* like him." Darcy eyed me evenly.

"I said I don't *know* him. I'm sure he's an okay guy."

"Well, good news, then, Elsie!" Darcy said. "He's available!" The girls erupted into peals of laughter.

"Let's call him over," Darcy said.

I rolled my eyes. "That's okay. I'll save you the trouble." I got up, picked up my tray and walked over to his table.

The girls' jaws dropped. I felt their eyes bore into my back. Martin was so involved in his book that he didn't notice me until I was standing right in front of him. *Social suicide, here I come.* "Hi, Martin," I said. "Can I eat with you?"

FOUR

"Tell me everything!"

Lani's timing was terrible. She called the moment I walked in after my first day at Harbin Springs Middle School. I didn't particularly feel like chatting about my experience as Darcy's Dumpster.

"C'mon, Elsa! Tell me all about your new school! Is it great?"

I sighed. "Great" wasn't the word that sprang to mind. "It's okay," I said. No use reliving every hideous little detail, right?

Try telling that to Lani.

"Details, details!" she squealed. "Are the girls nice?"

I sank into Grandma's sofa. "Sure, in a claw-your-eyes-out kind of way," I said. "Let's put it this way: The Slice Girls are alive and well at Horror Springs Middle School."

Lani gasped. *"Really?* Maybe every school has a Snotty Girl quota to fill. Wasn't anyone even halfway cool?"

I thought a second. "Yeah. My language arts teacher. He's really smart. And I ate lunch with a nice guy named Martin. He's on the baseball team, but only because his mother makes him play. He said the coach took pity on him and lets him warm the bench. In other words, he's the school geek, which means he's the only one I have anything in common with."

"What did you talk about?"

"Oh, I don't know. . . . We have a field trip on Wednesday; my language arts class is going to some printing plant to see how books are made, and he asked if I wanted to be his partner . . . you know, ride together on the bus, eat lunch together, that kind of thing. I told him sure. Then he got me up to speed about the school pecking order. This too-cool, ultra-snotty girl named Darcy is, like, the queen of seventh grade. Jade is her lady-in-waiting, and Carter and Jen are stupid servant girls who orbit around her."

"Shut *up!"* Lani squealed. "Just like the Slice Girls!"

"Right. Martin says sometimes when he looks like he's reading, he's actually watching how people act and making mental notes. He's thinking there's a book waiting to be written."

"He likes to write?" Lani asked, sounding suspicious.

"Yeah."

"Uh-oh. He really *is* a geek," she concluded grimly.

"I thought we already covered that, Lani."

"Okay, Elsa, here's the thing: You need to cut Martin loose."

I rolled my eyes. "He's the only one at school who was nice to me today," I said.

"Elsa! Seventh grade is every girl for herself." Lani sounded like a commander giving orders before sending troops into battle. "If you let yourself get labeled as Madame Geekstress right off the bat, you're doomed for the rest of the year. Maybe this could affect your entire life!"

Triple-L. Larger-than-Life Lani was in classic drama-queen form. "Well, what do *you* suggest I do?"

She shot off her answer like a bullet. "Suck up to Darcy," she said firmly. "Just for a few days, to get her off your back. Be nice to her until she gets bored and moves on to some other poor girl to sink her poison fangs into. By that time, you'll have a feel for the scene, and you can start to make some *real* friends."

I frowned. "What if *Martin* is a real friend?"

"Oh, Elsa." The tone of Lani's voice was exactly like when she tried to teach me how to dive off the high dive. (I didn't do it.) "You've got the rest of your life to have *real* friends. For now, you have to make nice with popular girls who can get you through seventh grade without your ego getting sliced and diced."

"I don't know, Lani. . . ."

"Trust me, Elsa. Otherwise, you're dead meat." She paused for effect. "Martin," she said gravely, "is social suicide."

❂

I walked into the kitchen and was getting my homework books out of my backpack when I heard a light jangling sound. I must have knocked something off the table. I bent down to scoop it up from the floor.

Weird. . . .

It was that necklace again, the gold locket with the heart.

"You again?" I said to the necklace. "Where did *you* come from?"

I shrugged. I put it back on the table, in case Grandma looked for it later. I'd have to remember to tell her I'd seen it. But right now, I had other things on my mind.

✿

I know it sounds whacked, but I was desperate enough to try to follow Lani's advice.

The next morning, I picked out my most Darceyesque outfit and attempted to brush my hair into the flowing locks that the clique had perfected . . . a major effort for me. I made a conscious effort to look friendly but cool as I walked to school. Then doom struck. Martin was the first person I saw.

"Hi, Elsa!" He was bounding toward me with his arms swinging by his sides and his eyes buried under his hair. "Want to walk to Mr. Wright's class with me?"

"Uh . . ." *Social suicide. Social suicide.* He'd said it himself! "I'd love to, Martin, but I have to stop by my locker. See you in class, okay?"

"I don't mind waiting."

Groan. "It'll take me a while. I'm still getting the knack of the lock, and then I have to drop off some new-student forms at the office."

"New-student forms?" He looked suspicious. My heart thudded. If this was the price of fitting in, I was starting to feel seriously bankrupt. "Okay," Martin finally said. "I thought we could meet before the field trip tomorrow."

"Right . . . about that . . ." I gazed down at the floor. "I'll probably get to school late, so you don't have to wait for me. Just sit with whoever is already there."

"No problem," he muttered as a mixture of hurt and resignation flashed in his dark eyes. He brushed back a lock of hair and walked away.

Mission accomplished, I thought. *So why do I feel so lousy?*

"Hi, Elsa!"

I turned toward the sound of the sunny, friendly voice. It was the redhead from Darcy's clique. I couldn't remember her name. "Hi . . . ," I said nervously.

"Carter," she said. "My name's Carter." She blushed. "Kind of a boy's name, I know. We met yesterday in the lunchroom."

"Right. I remember. Hope I didn't seem unfriendly by changing seats." I smiled and blushed slightly.

"Not at all." She leaned in close and whispered, "Darcy was being *such* a witch!"

I sighed, feeling a little more relaxed, and we started walking together toward my locker.

"True, Darcy and I are good enough friends," Carter said, "but she is *totally* stuck up."

I giggled. "Totally," I agreed.

"Ever since she made the cheerleading squad, she thinks she's all that," Carter said. "Plus, her dad is this big Hollywood producer." She twirled a finger in the air, a mock "Whoopee!" "She has, like, this total attitude," Carter continued. "She is *so* fake. Everything about her."

I nodded. "Yeah . . . the highlights are a little Miss America," I said, warming to the subject. "And those nails? I bet she spends more on her nails than my dad spent on my braces."

Carter nodded vigorously, holding her hand against her mouth as she giggled. "And that whole French manicure is *so* ten minutes ago. She's just trying to impress Eric. He's the pitcher on the baseball team. Like Eric cares about *her*. He's in eighth grade! Plus, he *so* thinks she's fake, but she's all in his face during break. *'Oh, Eric! You pitched so good last night at the game!'* " Her Darcy imitation was high and breathy.

"Guys hate that," I said, turning the corner toward my locker with Carter by my side. "My mom always said guys like it best when you play it cool and let them come to you."

"So," Carter asked as I opened my locker and pulled out my books, "did you have a boyfriend at your old school?"

I smiled and shook my head. "Nope," I said. "Once, in the lunchroom, I spilled chocolate milk all over a cute guy named Brent, and he nicknamed me Sludge. The name kinda stuck."

Carter laughed. "Well," she said, "I hope you don't think *I'm* a snob just because I hang around with Darcy sometimes."

"No," I said with a smile. "I think you're pretty cool."

Carter tossed her red hair over her shoulder. "*I think,*" she said, "we're going to be really good friends."

✪

The rest of the school day went pretty smoothly; I even sat with Darcy and her clique during lunch, and although Carter acted nice to her, she sneaked smiles to remind me that we were on the same side. I noticed Martin glancing up at me from his book a couple of times as we ate. I looked away before making eye contact.

Later, Carter asked me if I wanted to be her partner during the field trip.

"Sure."

Carter smiled. It *looked* like a sweet enough smile. . . .

✪

Mr. Wright was checking attendance as I stepped onto the bus the next morning.

"Find your partner and have a seat." Mr. Wright already sounded weary.

I walked slowly through the bus, looking for Carter's trademark red hair. I saw her sitting behind Darcy, Jade and Jen, who were all squeezed into a two-person seat. "Hi!" I said, scooting into the seat beside Carter.

Darcy suddenly spun around.

"Hi, *Sludge,*" she hissed. Carter giggled with her hand over her mouth. Oh no. . . .

I tried to shake it off. "So," I said cheerfully, "you heard my old nickname?"

"Yes, Elsie . . . I mean *Sludge*. I heard a few other things, too."

I cringed. "What do you mean?"

"I heard you've got, like, a major prob with my . . . oh, what did you call them? My Miss America highlights."

I looked at Carter, who turned her head and looked out the window, still stifling giggles.

"I think your hair's really pretty," I lied. "I didn't mean anything by it."

"*Sure.*" Darcy rolled her eyes dramatically. "Well, *Sludge,* since my hair is such a problem for you, why don't you sit far, far away from it? Looks like some seats are available in the back. *Way* back."

Carter looked smug and patted Darcy on the back. "I'm sure Elsa didn't really mean it," she said, tossing me an icy stare as Jade and Jen giggled.

I had no choice. I started walking toward the back of the bus, away from their snickers and stares. I paused as I passed Martin, who was sitting alone, but he looked out the window when he saw me. I kept walking to the back. *Way* back.

FIVE

Three days down. Three zillion to go. It was ten p.m. Wednesday night and I already felt like I'd endured a lifetime of torture at Horror Springs Middle School. I'd followed Lani's advice, and where had it gotten me? I slogged through the field trip, ignored by one and all. If my *eeeewww* factor had been any higher, the janitor would have tossed me out with the leftover mystery meat.

I'd put up a brave front for Dad and Grandma so far, but now it felt like the whole "everything's fine" charade was crashing down on my head. I was miserable and exhausted.

I fell onto my bed and looked at my dolphin posters. Stupid, babyish dolphins. What a loser I was. Those posters were coming down tomorrow.

I glanced at Mom's smiling face in the pictures on my bedside table. Everything had been so easy for her when she was my age. I felt like her trophies and neatly framed certificates were mocking me.

I started sobbing into my pillow. *It's all your fault, Mom! How could you do this to me?*

I wiped my tearstained eyes with my sheet, then clenched it with my fist and rolled around until I was swaddled so tightly, I could barely move.

"It's not fair!" I cried out loud, the words rumbling up my throat and spilling out like lava. "Your life was perfect. You didn't have any problems."

I sobbed into my pillow for a minute or two and then, still wrapped in my sheet, I turned to face my ceiling. Which is when I heard the tinkling of metal on the floor. The sound came from right beside my bed, as if I'd knocked something from the sheets.

I leaned over and squinted at the floor. That's when I saw a necklace lying in a small heap. I reached down and scooped it up.

Even through my tears, I could tell it was that weird necklace. Why did it keep turning up?

I snuggled into my bed and held the necklace close to my face, peering at the little etched heart. Overhead, my plastic stars were glowing softly, casting golden light into the shadows of the room. I touched the picture on my bedside table. . . . Mom holding me from behind, both of us laughing, me safe in her arms . . .

My tears started flowing again. "Why can't I have my mom?" I whimpered softly. "And what's up with this dumb necklace?"

"Dumb necklace, huh? A lot *you* know."

I gasped. The female voice was coming from beside me in the bed. *Beside me . . . in the bed . . .* I squeezed my eyes shut, too terrified to look. Someone was beside me in the bed!

As scared as I was, I had to know who was with me. And how she had gotten into my room—into my bed!—without my knowing.

My eyes flew open and I saw her. *My mom.*

I know what you're thinking. Here I was, crying in bed and moaning to my dead mother, missing her so badly that I suddenly sensed she was there, sitting beside me on the bed.

Wrong.

She really *was* there, smiling at me, with her light brown hair falling softly against my neck as her arms gently enfolded me. I wouldn't have believed it if I hadn't been there myself, and for a minute, I almost didn't. "If this is a dream," I murmured, "please don't let me wake up."

"It's not a dream, honey," Mom said, squeezing me closer to her.

I didn't want the moment to end, but I was too freaked out to just lie there. I flung off the covers and sat up. I stared at her. I even poked her a little.

Mom was still there. She smiled and held the palm of her hand against my cheek.

"It's me, babe," she said. "It's Mom."

I blinked again and again. Still there.

"Mom . . . *Mom!* How can you be here? *Oh, Mom!*"

I fell into her arms, pressing salty tears into her nightgown. "Is it really you? Are you really here?"

"I'm really here, sweetie. Actually, I always am. I'm like the stars on your ceiling. When you're sleeping, I'm plain to see, but when you're awake, I just blend in."

"Am I sleeping now?"

"No. Usually that's the only time I can talk to you and remind you I'm still watching over you. But I got special permission for this visit."

I shook my head slowly from side to side, still trying to take it all in. "Special permission? From who?"

"You know," Mom said casually, pointing her index finger skyward. "The Big Guy."

"Is he blending in, too?" I asked, looking up.

"Yup. Always remember: Just because you can't see us doesn't mean we aren't there."

I frowned. "But what good does blending in do if I can't touch you and talk to you?" I asked. "Oh, Mom, I miss you so much! You just don't know how much I miss you!"

"I *do* know, honey," Mom said. "I really do. And you're right: From *my* perspective, we're still together. But from *your* perspective, I just dropped off the face of the earth. Total bummer, right?"

I nodded. "Totally. I know it sounds warped to be mad at you for dying, but Mom, sometimes that's how I feel. And then I feel bad for feeling mad." I dabbed tears from my eyes. "I'm sorry, Mom. I'm sorry you died, and I'm sorry I'm mad, and I'm tired of being sad, and nothing's right or fair anymore and . . ."

"I know, baby, I know. And you know me: When I think something is unfair, I won't pipe down until I try to *make* it fair." She gave me the smile she used to reserve for when she was sharing a secret. "My stubbornness is causing a bit of a stir. Apparently, I've set a new standard up there for being a world-class pest." She leaned closer, whispering now: "That's why I got special permission to visit."

"For how long?" I asked, terrified at the thought of her evaporating before my eyes.

"Just for a bit," she said. "But it's okay. Remember, even when you can't see me, I'm still here, just blending in."

"Not good enough," I groused, then smiled in spite of myself. "I guess you're not the only stubborn one in the family."

Mom winked. "That's my girl. But as long as I'm here . . . in the flesh, so to speak . . . let's make the most of my visit. I want to help you stop being so unhappy at school."

I sighed. "That's a pretty tall order, Mom, even from you . . . or the Big Guy . . . or whoever. I'm not like you, all pretty and popular and perfect. I'm a mess."

Mom laughed, her eyes sparkling.

"Pretty? Popular? Perfect? You're describing Lisa Tilden, honey, not me."

"Who's Lisa Tilden?"

Mom scrunched her nose. "My Lisa was your Darcy. The snooty cheerleader who always managed to make me feel like a loser. Every school has a Lisa or a Darcy. And I'll tell you a secret: From my new perspective, I'm seeing that their lives aren't so perfect, either. They aren't evil, they're just confused and insecure. They think if they knock you off balance, they'll stand a little taller."

"But everybody loved you," I protested. "How could anyone have made your life miserable?"

"Let's see: nose too long, legs too skinny, hair too thin, mouth too loud . . ." I giggled as she reeled off her list.

"None of those things are true," I insisted. "And even if they *were* true, those are the things that make you . . . *you*."

Mom tousled my hair. "Exactly, sweetie. At your age, you can't win. I think the trick is to be a loser on your own terms. Find one or two really good friends—people who care about you for all the right reasons—and stay true to yourself. Forget Darcy's rules and stick to your own plan. Then even if you don't win in the short run, you've got it nailed over the long haul."

She raised her eyebrows. "And don't even *think* about tearing down your dolphin posters, young lady. I love your dolphins!"

I pouted dramatically, an expression that always made Mom laugh. "But I need help," I said firmly. "Stop blending in and stay right here with me."

Mom pouted back at me. "Now, *that*," she said, poking me playfully in the chest, "would be a *major* infraction of the rules. Even *I* can't pull that off."

"You can't leave me again, Mom. Please don't."

She gathered me in her arms. "Don't worry, sweetie," she whispered. "I'll help you, I promise."

She put her hands on my shoulders and looked me squarely in the eye. "What I'm about to propose is way, *way* irregular. Unprecedented, even." She looked a little nervous. "But there you have it."

My eyebrows knitted together as I studied her curiously. "What are we talking about?"

Mom cleared her throat, sounding official. "You turn thirteen in a little over a month. May eleventh."

"And . . . ?"

She squeezed her hand around my fist, which was still clutching the weird necklace. "Here's the plan: For the next month, until your thirteenth birthday, I hereby grant you do-over power."

I laughed out loud. "Do-over power," I repeated. "And what exactly might that be?"

"Well . . . I'm kinda making up the rules as I go along," Mom confessed, "but here's how it'll work . . . I hope . . . if we're lucky. . . ." She glanced skyward as if to make sure she had permission from the Big Guy to proceed.

"Mom! You're making me nervous!"

She shrugged. "Well . . . what's the worst that can happen?" She cleared her throat again. "Hopefully, we won't have to find out. Okay, the plan: For the next month, whenever you're having a tough time . . . say, you spill your chocolate milk in the lunchroom again, or tell a joke and no one laughs, just rub the necklace you're holding and say, 'Do-over.' "

"The necklace! I wondered why this necklace kept popping up. . . ."

"My mom gave it to me when I was right around your age," Mom said. "She told me the women in our family are stronger than we know, and that this necklace would help me tap into my strength. I wore the necklace every day for the rest of seventh grade, and somehow, it made my life easier. Nothing magical happened; I just felt more confident wearing it. Then I kind of outgrew it. I didn't really need it anymore, you know? It was just a necklace, and I felt I was ready to take on the world without it. I put it away . . . but I had a hunch it would come in handy later."

I shook my head slowly. "I'm talking to my mom, who happens to be *dead,* and she's giving me a necklace, which happens to have some magical power," I muttered, trying somehow to make sense of what was happening.

Mom ran her cool fingers through my hair. "Here's the deal," she said. "When you rub this locket and say 'Do-over,' the world rewinds for ten seconds. Then you can replay the scene any way you want."

I shook my head again as the total craziness of the whole situation started sinking in. "The world rewinds . . . ," I repeated numbly.

"For ten seconds," Mom repeated. "Just long enough to fix an embarrassing moment. For one month only."

"How many times can I do a do-over?" I asked, deciding that since this night had veered hopelessly into Loco Land, I might as well play along.

Mom shrugged. "As I said, I'm kinda making up the rules as I go along. So here's the deal: You need a do-over? You've got it. Between now and May eleventh, you get as many as you want."

Loco Land seemed like a pretty awesome place. "And what if I don't like my do-over any better than I liked things the first time around?" I asked.

Mom shrugged cheerfully. "Do it over again!" she said. "No one will know what's happening except you . . . and me, of course. Everyone else will think they're experiencing that moment for the first time."

I held out the palm of my hand like a police officer signaling someone to freeze. "Okay, look," I said. "*Assuming* I'm not dreaming, and *assuming* I'm not insane, and *assuming* a lightning bolt doesn't crash on my head when I say 'Do-over,' which, incidentally, will make me sound like a complete idiot if it doesn't work . . . *assuming* all that . . . can I tell Dad and Grandma what's going on?"

Mom bit her bottom lip. "You still have free will, honey," she said. "I can't control what you do or say. But don't you think Dad and Grandma have enough on their plates without worrying that you've gone certifiable on them?"

I gasped as the thought of Dad and Grandma suddenly formed clearly in my mind. "Dad and Grandma!" I sputtered. "They need to see you! Oh, Mom, they miss you so much. Let me go get them!"

Mom shook her head sadly. "I can't, honey," she said. "Getting permission to come to *you* required absolutely all my persuasive powers. There's no way I can show myself to Dad or Grandma . . . and maybe that's for the best."

My mouth gaped. "How can you say that?" I demanded. "Of course they want to see you!"

"I know, honey, but they're doing a great job processing their grief and moving forward. I don't want to interfere with that. But remember: I'm always watching out for them. I'm blending into their lives just like I blend into yours."

I searched her eyes. "Will I see you again after tonight?"

Mom kissed my forehead, then took the necklace from my hand and clasped it behind my neck. "I'll visit you in your dreams, I promise," she said. "And who knows . . . as stubborn as I am, I might be able to arrange a follow-up visit in the flesh. If not, just talk to me anytime you need me, and know I'll be listening. I can't promise to make a chandelier shake to let you know I'm close by, but I'll be there. Cross my heart."

I traced the outline of her face with my finger. "I believe you . . . ," I said slowly, ". . . yet I also believe that I am totally nuts."

She laughed and hugged me tightly. "Then let's just cut to the chase: Remember I love you, remember I'm always here . . . and remember to use your do-overs wisely. The only person you can change is yourself." She kissed my cheeks. "Be true to yourself, Elsa," she said. "That's all I ask."

And then she disappeared.

Well . . . blended in.

SIX

Do-Over Day One

Sunlight was already streaming through my bedroom window when the radio started blasting right on cue: 6:30 a.m. Time to face another disastrous day at Horror Springs Middle School.

But I didn't care. I actually woke up smiling. I'd had my best night's sleep since Mom had died. The kind of sleep you have when your mom is perfectly fine and snoozing in the next room.

What a great dream.

I know what you're thinking: It should be a bummer to dream about your dead mom, right? All heavy and depressing? Wrong. It was the best dream. I didn't even care that it wasn't real. For a few magical moments, I'd had my mom back, all warm and funny and lavender-scented. She'd been right there with me. She'd been with me in my dream. At this point, I'd take my mom any way I could get her.

The weather forecast on the radio matched my mood.

"As you're rising and shining this morning, folks, look forward to a beautiful day with sunny skies and a high in the midseventies, with just a few puffy clouds rolling in later this afternoon," the deejay said.

Appropriate.

I felt something cool on my neck and gasped as I realized what it was: the necklace.

Was it possible . . . ?

"Do-over," I said haltingly as I rubbed the locket.

Strange . . . Suddenly, the radio was making some kind of weird garbly noise, like a tape rewinding. Then . . .

"As you're rising and shining this morning, folks, look forward to a beautiful day with sunny skies and a high in the midseventies, with just a few puffy clouds rolling in later this afternoon."

My heart skipped a beat.

"Do-over," I whispered, nervously rubbing the locket.

Again, the funny garbly sound, then . . .

"As you're rising and shining this morning, folks, look forward to a beautiful day . . ."

Oh. My. God.

Omigod!

I covered over my eyes and squealed under my breath. No way!

"Do-over?" I squeaked.

Weird garbly sound.

"As you're rising and shining this morning, folks . . ."

I bolted straight up in bed. "Mom?" I called out frantically. "Mom, are you there? Wasn't that whole ghost visit thing a dream? Mom, answer me!"

Nothing.

". . . and expect a delay if you're traveling on Washington Road this morning," the deejay continued, "where a three-car wreck is tying up traffic. Only minor injuries are reported, none serious enough for a trip to the hospital."

I rubbed the locket. "Do-over!"

Weird garbly sound.

". . . and expect a delay if you're traveling on Washington Road this morning, where a three-car wreck is tying up traffic . . ."

My jaw dropped. "Whoa . . . ," I muttered.

Was this possible? Had Mom really held me in her arms the night before? Had she really clasped this necklace around my neck and given me do-over power? It couldn't be true. No way. Dad would explain this to me, because obviously there was a logical explanation and only Dad could explain it and I really had to talk to Dad RIGHT NOW, and . . .

"DAAAADDDD!"

My voice echoed through the house as I jumped out of my bed, tore down the stairs and ran into the kitchen.

Dad and Grandma jumped up from the table.

"Elsa!" Dad said. "What in the world . . ."

"It's Mom . . . ," I said breathlessly. "Dad, I know it's nuts, but Mom came to see me last night."

My eyes quickly scanned their faces. Grandma seemed strangely calm, but Dad looked downright terrified.

"Honey . . . ," he said in barely a whisper.

Just then, Mom's words floated back into my head: *"Don't you think Dad and Grandma have enough on their plates without worrying that you've gone certifiable on them?"*

I frantically rubbed my locket and yelped, *"Do-over!"*

Wow. . . . I watched the past ten seconds rewind before my eyes. Everything was happening in reverse. Even my actions, but it was weird. My feet stayed planted on the floor in the kitchen, but I watched a transparent, ghostlike version of me moving backward. The real me just stood there and watched it happen—the transparent me hurtling back toward the stairs, and Dad and Grandma inching down into their seats at the kitchen table. It was like pressing the Rewind button on a VCR.

"DAAAADDDD!" I heard myself screaming, reliving the moment I had just rewound. At that instant, the real me and the transparent me blended back into one.

Once again, I ran into the kitchen and saw Dad and Grandma jump up from the table. "Elsa!" Dad said. "What in the world . . ."

"Uh . . ." I paused to catch my breath. This was really happening. Dad had no idea why I'd just run screaming into the kitchen. It was as if the past ten seconds had never happened. Now I needed a reason for running and screaming into the kitchen. "I saw a spider in my room," I said, trying to calm down.

Dad rolled his eyes. "I thought you were on fire!" he said, visibly relieved.

"Sorry," I said. My thoughts were still spinning. "Spiders just kinda creep me out, you know?"

Dad looked skeptical. "No, I don't know," he said. "This, from the kid who put a lizard in her ear on a dare?"

I scrunched my shoulders. "Go figure."

Dad and Grandma exchanged puzzled glances, and I felt a sudden burst of energy.

"Hey, Dad, Grandma," I said, running toward the refrigerator. "Do you guys like scrambled eggs?"

On a whim, I pulled a carton of eggs from the fridge door. "Here goes nothing," I said, then held the carton upside down over my head. A dozen eggs came crashing down on me, soaking my hair with goo.

Dad and Grandma were stunned. They stood there watching egg yolk dribble down my face with their jaws dropped open. I giggled and rubbed my locket. *This better still work . . .* , I thought.

"Do-over!"

The eggs defied gravity and pulled themselves from my hair back into the carton. I placed the carton in the fridge.

"This, from the kid who put a lizard in her ear on a dare?" Dad said, repeating what he'd said ten seconds before.

It worked!

"Yeah, well, I'm full of surprises," I said, now officially on a roll. "Speaking of surprises, I've decided to quit school and join the Peace Corps. I'm leaving in the morning for Tibet."

Dad yawned and tousled my hair. "Yeah, honey, good

luck with that," he said, going back to the table. "Take the spider, too, will ya?"

I huffed grumpily. That reaction didn't even merit a do-over.

Oh, well. The important thing was that the power really worked. Now, what could I do with it?

SEVEN

Dad finished his coffee and went upstairs to get dressed for work.

"Have a good day," he called a few minutes later.

Now *that's a distinct possibility*, I thought with a grin.

It was beginning to dawn on me that my do-overs had the power to make my life nothing short of perfect . . . if I was smart enough to maximize my opportunity.

The front door shut as I returned to the kitchen after dressing.

Good. I had Grandma all to myself. If I was going to get some serious mileage out of my do-overs, I needed a crash course in perfection. I needed a crash course in Mom.

"Grandma," I said, trying to sound casual as I washed down some oatmeal with orange juice. "Tell me what Mom was like at my age."

Grandma glanced at me quickly, as if I'd startled her, but

she cleared her throat and tried to look nonchalant. "Hmmm," she said with the fake cheerfulness she used when talking about Mom. "What do you want to know?"

"For starters, what was she like when she was a kid? What were her hobbies?"

"Well . . ." Grandma tapped a finger on the tabletop. Then she waved her hand through the air as she decided what she wanted to say. "Well, she was brilliant, for one thing."

"Brilliant?"

Grandma got a dreamy look in her eyes as she gazed out the window. "Brilliant," she repeated, this time sounding genuinely cheery. "You mom was so smart, from the time she was a tiny baby. I remember thinking when she was little, 'How will the world ever be big enough for that brain of hers?' "

Grandma looked back at me and laughed in embarrassment. "Moms think like that," she said, leaning in close like she was sharing a secret. "But your mom really *was* smart. Never had to study, really. Just paid attention in class and soaked it all up. She was interested in almost everything, so she enjoyed learning about new things. In fact, she always got sidetracked doing her homework. She'd be studying spelling words, for instance, and she'd want to look the words up and learn more about them. Spelling them correctly wasn't enough."

Yep, that was my mom. She was the same way with my homework. "Mom," I would say in frustration, "I don't need a crash course on the reign of Queen Victoria. I just need to know how to spell 'monarch.' " I smiled at the memory.

"Your mom even started a school newspaper when she was around your age," Grandma continued. "It was only a few pages long, but her flair for writing was evident even then." Grandma looked dreamy again. "Brilliant."

I wrinkled my brow. "But aren't eggheads kind of . . . you know . . . nerdy?" I giggled and leaned closer to Grandma. "Was Mom a nerd?"

"I beg your pardon!" Grandma teased. "The women in our family never mask their intelligence for anyone. Your mother was always being asked to write the school play or come up with funny photo captions for the school yearbook. She was smart, but she was also funny and a pleasure to be around." Grandma rubbed my cheek. "Like you."

Hmmm . . . suddenly, it all seemed to make perfect sense. *Be true to yourself, Elsa,"* Mom had told me. Well, *Mom* was brilliant, and *I* was Mom's daughter. Maybe being true to myself meant being like Mom. Maybe Horror Springs Middle School was about to meet the most brilliant seventh grader to walk its halls since . . . since . . . well, since Mom.

I finished breakfast and kissed Grandma. "Thanks," I said. "I want to be just like Mom."

Grandma smiled but looked worried.

"I need to get going," I said, reaching for my backpack.

Grandma took my arm and looked deeply into my eyes. "Elsa," she said intently, "you're a lot like your mom. But you need to be your own person, *on your own terms,* and you already possess everything you need to do that. There's only one Elsa Alden, and I wouldn't have it any other way." She squeezed my arm. "Neither would your mom."

I nodded, grabbed my gear and ran out the door.

Grandma meant well, but I knew deep down that being Mom was far superior to being Elsa Alden.

And now Mom had given me the power to make that happen.

◐

My mind raced as I walked along the sidewalk. How exactly should I begin my new do-over-powered life?

First, I thought, *I'm gonna have a little fun.*

An automatic sprinkler was watering the grass at the house next door. It was a little thing, but I loved running through sprinklers. I dumped my backpack on the sidewalk and ran across the lawn. A dozen streams of water rained down on me from all directions. I shrieked in delight, stretching my arms wide. I held out my tongue to let the water drop into my mouth.

I giggled. I hadn't done anything like that since I was six years old. But time was running out. . . .

Reluctantly, I rubbed my locket and said, "Do-over."

Now I was running through the sprinklers backward. Again, there was the strange sensation of standing in one spot while I watched the ghost figure of myself running backward as drops of water bounced *off* me instead of *onto* me. I kept running backward until I was on the edge of the yard where I'd started, high and dry.

"Awesome."

I kept walking and saw a cute guy coming in my direction, probably heading for the high school. Before, I could never even bring myself to look such a hottie in the eye, but now . . . I had nothing to lose.

"Excuse me," I said as we passed. He stopped walking and stared at me. "Would you do me a big favor?" I asked. "I've never been kissed before, and I figure now is as good a time as any. Would you mind kissing me? Nothing too mushy; just a little peck."

He jerked his head away from me and narrowed his eyes. "What are you, some kind of freak?" he said.

Thanks a lot.

I rubbed my locket. "Do-over."

Now I watched as he and my ghost self walked backward, away from each other. Then that weird merging of my ghost self and my real self at the instant that time started ticking again. As we walked toward each other, I tried a new approach. "Hey, big shot," I said. "It wouldn't kill you to say hello, would it? Get over yourself, will ya?"

"What are you, some kind of freak?" he said.

Hmmmph. No imagination. Hottie or not, he definitely wasn't my type.

I rubbed my locket.

"Do-over."

This time, when we passed each other, we kept walking.

Missed your chance, I thought playfully. *Your loss.*

What happened next made me realize that this power didn't have to be all about me. As I continued walking, I saw a toddler run through his front yard, then cry when he tripped over a rake.

I rubbed my locket. "Do-over."

The toddler ran backward instead of forward, hurtling back ten seconds in time. As he headed toward the rake, I ran over and scooped him up in time to undo the fall. He peered up at me, then burst into tears.

"Now, *that's* gratitude," I said playfully, smoothing his hair. I picked up the rake and leaned it against his house, then continued walking to school.

"Thanks . . . ," his mother called to me from the front porch.

So. This really was happening. I had just undone a skinned knee. What else was I capable of?

"Okay, Mom," I said under my breath. "You got me into this. You are watching out for me . . . right?"

I quickened my stride and took a deep breath of the balmy morning air. One way or another, seventh grade was definitely about to take a turn in a new direction. I'd tried blending in, and that was a disaster. Now it was time to stand out.

EIGHT

Carter was at her locker when I reached mine.

"Oh, hi, Elsa," she cooed in a gaggy saccharine tone. "Did you enjoy the field trip yesterday? Hate it that we couldn't be partners."

I opened my locker and started digging through it. "Right," I said. "Hate it that you ratted me out to Darcy."

Carter gasped. "As *if*!" she huffed. "Somebody else must have overheard us. *I* didn't say a word! Besides, I thought she'd consider it a compliment that you think she looks like Miss America. That *is* what you said . . . right?"

"Something like that," I muttered.

Carter's locker door clanged shut. "The good news," she said, "is that Darcy totally forgives you."

I brushed the back of my hand along my forehead. "*Whew!*" I said sarcastically.

My do-over power had given me the nerve to say exactly

what was on my mind, knowing I could unsay it if necessary. It felt great to have such confidence. And rather than acting miffed, Carter seemed kind of . . . impressed. As I started to walk away, she quickened her pace to keep up with me.

"Wait up!" she called.

The new and improved Elsa, I thought with a smile.

In fact, while I was at it . . .

Carter was still trotting along when I decided to make a detour to the school office and see Grouchy Office Lady.

I stuck my head in the office. Mrs. Stiffle didn't even look up.

"Oh, Mrs. Stiffle," I said in a singsong voice.

No response.

"Hey! Stiffle!" I barked so loudly that she jumped. "Look alive! And while you're at it, turn that frown upside down, Grouchy Office Lady."

The look that swept over Mrs. Stiffle's face was gradual and so satisfying that I hated to cut the moment short. Her eyebrows rose first, then her jaw dropped and her hands balled up into tight little fists, and . . .

I rubbed my locket. "Do-over."

Ten-second rewind. Darn. It almost would have been worth it not to undo the moment. But I was confident, not suicidal, so this time, I bypassed the office and kept walking to class.

I took long strides, trying to look important. It must have worked, because Carter was breathlessly running behind me.

We walked into the classroom, where Darcy, Jen and Jade were already hovering in the doorway. "Love the nails,

Jade," I said in a too-cool tone of voice, curling my lip as I glanced down at the cotton-candy color. "Did you find that shade in the toddler section of the cosmetics counter?"

I was going to snatch the moment back, but although Jade blushed, Darcy, Jen and Carter looked on in total admiration. *This* they admired? I was sorry for Jade's sake, but I'd obviously stumbled onto something big.

And if they thought *snotty* was cool, just wait until I added *brilliant* to the mix.

The bell rang and Mr. Wright waved us in from the doorway. "Seats, everybody," he said. "We've got a lot to cover."

I smiled shyly at Martin as I passed him, but he looked away. I didn't blame him for being mad. But things would change when he realized how smart I was. Soon everybody in the whole school would want to be my friend.

"Ladies and gentlemen," Mr. Wright said, propping himself on the edge of his desk, "today we're going to start reading a novel written by a woman who lived just a couple of states away. It's a Southern book with a Southern sensibility, so I think you'll all be able to relate to the dialect, the characters, the setting. But what I find most fascinating about *To Kill a Mockingbird* is its universality. Because Harper Lee taps into the most basic elements of humanity, it's a book that any person, from any spot on the globe, can relate to. The essence, of course, of a great novel."

I smiled and rubbed my locket. "Do-over."

Suddenly, Mr. Wright was talking backward gibberish. Yes! It was working.

". . . so I think you'll all be able to relate to the dialect, the characters, the setting," he said when the gibberish ended, picking up where he'd left off ten seconds earlier.

"Mr. Wright!" I called out, waving my arm in the air.

He looked startled but cleared his throat and said, "Elsa?"

"I agree that Southerners can easily relate to the book," I said, "but what I find most fascinating about *To Kill a Mockingbird* is its universality." Mr. Wright's jaw dropped ever so subtly. *Don't pour it on too thick*, I told myself, but I was on a roll. "I'm not sure I can put it into words, but Harper Lee somehow manages to tap into the most basic elements of humanity. It's a book that anybody anywhere can relate to . . . the essence of a great novel, don't you think?"

Mr. Wright stared at me as if I'd just grown a second head.

"Uh . . . ," he finally said, "you took the words right out of my mouth." His eyebrows knitted together. "You've already read the book, Elsa?"

I nodded, smiling primly.

Mr. Wright shifted his weight, like he was regaining his footing. "Good," he said a little nervously. "Good. Well, for those of you who *haven't* read it yet . . . I'm guessing that's everybody else . . . you're in for a treat. If you like horror movies, there's something in this book for you. If you like crime dramas, there's that as well. If you like suspense . . ."

I rubbed my locket. "Do-over."

Ten-second rewind.

". . . you're in for a treat," Mr. Wright said, picking up where he'd left off ten seconds earlier.

"Mr. Wright!" Up flew my hand.

The slightest trace of annoyance flashed across Mr. Wright's face. "Yes, Elsa," he said in a tight voice.

"Have you noticed that To Kill a Mockingbird is, like, equal parts horror movie, crime drama and suspense?"

This time, there was nothing subtle about it: Mr. Wright's mouth literally fell open.

"Wha-" he said, his voice trailing off.

"Oh, I'm sorry," I said sweetly. "I interrupted you. It's just hard to contain my enthusiasm. That's, like, my favorite book in the whole world."

Darcy slowly turned in her seat until her eyes locked with mine, one eyebrow arched in an upside-down **V**.

"I'm glad you like it, Elsa," Mr. Wright said, sounding a little flustered, "but let's save some surprises for the rest of the class."

"Yeah, Elsa," a voice called from two rows over. Everyone turned toward the sound. It was Martin, eyeing me with a steady gaze. "We wouldn't want everyone to know, for example, that Boo Radley is really a harmless old kook who saves Scout's life at the end. Or that Atticus loses his case."

It was a challenge, one that caught me off guard enough to forget my secret weapon. *Sorry, Martin,* I thought, *but you'll have to step aside as the smartest kid in the class. Survival of the fittest and all that . . .*

Mr. Wright clapped his palms together loudly. "Maybe we should start summer break a few weeks early. I'm feeling a little redundant up here." The class tittered and Mr. Wright rubbed the back of his neck. "Is there anyone in this class who *hasn't* read To Kill a Mockingbird?"

Slowly, hands started rising, until every one was up except Martin's and mine. Of course I hadn't read it! But who would know? School had just gotten a giant step easier . . . and with my new surefire mix of brains, snottiness and confidence, I was a giant step closer to fitting in.

✪

I continued to dazzle Horror Springs Middle School with my brilliance the rest of the morning. In math class, I'd wait for someone to give the correct answer, then say "Do-over" and blurt it out first. I suddenly knew gobs and gobs about fractions, proportions, percents and statistics. (And math was my worst subject!)

In social studies, I was an instant expert on ancient Indian civilizations. Sometimes, I would ask the teacher a question ("Mrs. Rivers, what do *you* think were the major cultural contributions of the Aztecs?"), then say "Do-over" and volunteer the information as if it was coming out of my own head. When Mrs. Rivers pointed out that the world map in our textbook was outdated, I asked for a few details, quickly said "Do-over" and then yammered on about the need for new textbooks, what with the USSR no longer existing and at least five African nations having changed their names since that map was made. (Then, yes, I named them.)

In art class, I asked Ms. Simmons periodically how she liked my sketches, then said "Do-over," erased what she didn't like and penciled in the new lines that reflected her taste.

"Elsa, those branches are awfully straight," Ms. Simmons said as I drew a tree. "Don't you think they'd look more realistic if you gave each one a unique shape and character?"

"As a matter of fact, I do," I replied. "Thanks for the suggestion!" I rubbed my locket. "Do-over."

Suddenly, the branches were perfectly shaped (well . . . make that *im*perfectly shaped) the first time around.

No need to burden my teachers with my amateurish work or unsophisticated answers if a ten-second rewind could give them exactly what they were looking for.

I had a little bit of trouble in science class; I blurted "Do-over!" and snatched other people's answers a couple of times before I had a chance to realize they were wrong. (Who knew that mitosis and meiosis are two different things?) But I just kept replaying each moment until I had my science teacher, Ms. Wilkins, convinced that I was the next Carl Sagan. (I hadn't even known who he was until I became an instant expert on his astronomy theories, thanks to Martin's contributions in class!)

It was a little off-topic, but one time, I pointed to an anatomical drawing on Ms. Wilkins' wall and asked her the name of one of the bones. When she told me, I rubbed my locket, said "Do-over," and then raised my hand and said, "By the way, Ms. Wilkins, do all primates have a maxilla?"

Just for fun.

Sure, I felt a few twinges of guilt. It wasn't really fair to snatch answers and ideas right out of people's mouths, but they were none the wiser. And I really *was* smart, right? Now I was just letting the world know it. I would never cheat on a test or anything; in fact, this new reputation was giving me lots of incentive to study harder so I wouldn't be exposed as a fraud. This was a *good* thing . . . right?

And best of all, it was working. People were noticing me. Jaws were dropping as brilliant answers spilled out of my mouth, one after another. I was the smartest kid in school, just like my mom had been. I hoped that if Mom was blending in, she was proud of me. How could she not be? I was downright perfect.

NINE

Darcy caught up with me in the lunch line after art class.

"Hey, Elsa, why don't you sit with us today?" she asked, trying to sound casual.

I smiled. Just like the new fringed shirts that everybody was wearing, I was suddenly in hot demand.

"Sure," I said, taking my tray and following her to the Popular Table.

"Gee, Elsa, you're like some kind of child progeny or something, aren't you?" Carter said as I pulled up a chair. I tried to hide my smile. Maybe I wasn't as smart as I was making everybody believe, but I knew the difference between *progeny* and *prodigy*.

I shrugged. "I guess I just retain information easily." Brilliant *and* modest!

Darcy's lip curled. "Well, you may be a brainiac, but you

sure don't know how to keep your clothes clean," she said, staring at the fringe on my shirt, which had dipped into my gravy. "Eeewww."

Uh-oh. I rubbed my locket. "Do-over!"

No gravy-stained fringe for me.

"I guess I just retain information easily," I repeated, lowering myself carefully—and stain-free—into my seat.

"You're even smarter than Martin!" Jen said admiringly.

"Smarter than *Martin?*" Jade replied. "She's smarter than the *teachers*."

"You may be the smartest person in the universe," Carter said slowly, as if she was making an observation of grave importance.

I waved a dismissive hand through the air. "No, really . . . ," I cooed. I felt like a movie star being fawned over on the red carpet at the Academy Awards. Autograph, anyone?

"Sit by me in study hall next period," Darcy said abruptly. "I need help with my math homework."

My muscles tensed. *That* could be a problem. It was one thing to steal other people's answers after they'd already said them. It was another thing to come up with answers on my own. I quickly changed the subject. "What's everybody doing this weekend?"

Carter grinned. "Darcy's going to see her dad, the Hollywood producer!"

"Your dad is a Hollywood producer?" I asked.

Darcy tossed her hair over her shoulder. "Like, *duh*."

The other girls giggled.

"Wow . . . ," I said, genuinely impressed. "Which movies has he made?"

Darcy looked a little uncomfortable. Her eyes dropped down to her lap for a split second; then she snapped her head up again.

"What do I look like, his agent?" she said with a sneer.

But I was curious. "Well, at least tell us one or two," I prodded.

"Yeah, Darcy!" Carter said, leaning closer to her. "Has he ever worked with any famous hotties?"

Darcy paused, then said, "It just so happens he's working with one this weekend. I can't name names, but let's just say you probably have his poster on your wall. I'll be on the set, of course."

"In Hollywood?" Carter asked breathlessly.

"No, Carter, in my backyard," Darcy said, making the rest of the clique titter. "*Yes*, in Hollywood. Now, don't go blabbing it all over town," she scolded, gently smoothing her pink-striped blouse. "I still have to be, like, *very discreet* about Dad's projects. If the paparazzi knew I was his daughter, they'd be all over me. I do *not* want my picture plastered all over some tacky tabloid."

"Really?" Carter asked, apparently genuinely stunned. Having her picture plastered all over some tacky tabloid seemed right up Darcy's alley.

"I don't *do* tacky," Darcy snapped in annoyance, pouting her glossy pink lips.

"Can you at least bring us back a picture?" Jen asked.

"Hmmmm," Darcy said, tapping her index finger against

her chin. "What a great idea. I'll just hang around the set like some starstruck groupie and make, like, a total fool of myself just so *you* can have a picture." She sneered. "Or not."

Darcy got up from her seat and walked her tray over to the conveyor belt.

She sure knew how to put people in their place. My popularity might have been growing, but no one was going to nudge Darcy from her throne. That seat was permanently reserved.

Not.

❂

A light breeze blew through my hair as I walked home from school that day.

"Elsa, wait up!"

I turned around. Uh-oh. . . . "Hi, Martin."

"I'm headed to your house," he said. "Well . . . your grandma's house."

"Why?"

"I do yard work for her on Thursday afternoons. So I guess we're going in the same direction."

My stomach tightened. "Guess so."

Martin slowed his pace to match mine. "What's the matter? Afraid one of your snob friends will spot you walking with a scrub?"

Ouch. "Look, Martin, I'm sorry if I hurt your feelings about the field trip," I said, and I meant it. "I'm the geeky new kid, okay? I'm just trying to fit in. Is that such a crime?"

Our shoes thumped against the sidewalk in unison. "Just trying to fit in?" he repeated with a laugh. "From where I sit, it looks like they'll be renaming the school in your honor any day now."

I frowned. "What's that supposed to mean?"

"Well, for one thing, it seems that you've had a brain transplant. With Albert Einstein as the donor."

"Very funny," I mumbled. "There's nothing wrong with being smart, you know."

"Granted," Martin said. "I like smart. *I* am smart. Not as smart as you, but then, who is? I mean, there's smart, and then there's freakishly smart."

My heart thumped faster. "Are you making fun of me?"

"No," he said. "I'm just confused about who you really are. It's hard to get a handle on you."

We walked on in silence. I didn't know what to say.

"Look," Martin finally said, "as smart as you are, don't forget to be smart about your friends. Intelligence doesn't carry much weight with Darcy and her clique, unless . . ."

I gazed at him defensively. "Unless what?"

"Unless they're trying to use you."

"Meaning what?"

He shrugged. "Take it from a guy who becomes very popular right before final exams."

My lips tightened. Darcy and her friends weren't using me. They really *were* impressed by how smart I was . . . weren't they? They thought it was cool, hanging out with the smartest girl in the school . . . didn't they?

Sure they did.

I thought.

I was relieved when we finally reached Grandma's house. Martin headed for the backyard as I climbed the front steps. "See ya, Martin," I said.

"See ya, smarty," he replied.

TEN

"Elsa, can we talk a minute, sweetie?"

Uh-oh. What now? It was that night. Dad walked in and sat on the edge of my bed just as I was snuggling under the covers.

"What's up, Dad?"

He folded his hands together and bounced them lightly against his knee.

"Well . . ." He seemed a little nervous. "I got a call from your principal today."

My eyes widened. Even under normal circumstances, it was impossible for a kid to hear those words without her insides turning to jelly.

"It seems you made quite an impression in school today," Dad continued. "*Quite* an impression."

My stomach felt all fluttery. "What do you mean?"

"The principal wants to talk to your former principal

and compare notes. He doesn't understand it, since the schools use the same curricula, but he thinks your old school must be more advanced than Harbin Springs." He paused. "Or maybe *you're* just far more advanced than anyone realized."

I gulped. "I've always done well in school, Dad," I said defensively. "I make the honor roll every semester! Why is everybody making such a big deal about me being a good student?"

Dad smiled. "Don't be upset, honey. I'm proud of you. And you're right, you've always done well in school. But the feedback I got today indicates that within the normal seventh-grade range, you're basically . . . off the charts." His eyebrows wrinkled together. "I'm not sure *how*. . . ."

"I don't know what everyone wants from me," I snapped, suddenly on the verge of tears.

"Honey, honey," Dad said soothingly, "I'm not criticizing you. I'm just trying to decide what's best for you. The principal thinks you should take some tests and maybe skip eighth grade next year."

What?

"No, Dad," I said decisively. "Bad idea." I was just starting to find my niche with seventh graders. Stick me in a grade with girls whose figures had already developed and I might as well tattoo "loser" on my forehead.

"But you don't want to be bored in school," Dad said. "You seem to know all the material your teachers are covering. I don't know *how*. . . . But the point is, I want you to be challenged."

Could a do-over help me now? I could turn back time

only ten seconds, not a whole day. What had I gotten myself into? And what was happening to my perfect day? Sometimes perfect is perfectly horrible but you don't know it yet.

"Dad, I happened to be extra-sharp today in school," I said with a hint of urgency in my voice. "I got lucky and knew the answers to some questions. Tomorrow, I might be brain-dead." Actually, there was a very good chance of that. "I don't want to skip eighth grade. Please, Dad?"

Dad rubbed my cheek. "Nobody's doing anything hasty," he assured me. "You haven't even finished a whole week in your new school yet. I think we should all take a deep breath and relax." He smiled. "Let's see how things go. Assuming you haven't discovered a cure for cancer by summertime, I'm guessing you're right where you're supposed to be."

I smiled and wrapped his hand in mine.

"We've had a lot of big changes lately, kiddo," he said, winking at me. "As long as we stick together, we'll do just fine."

ELEVEN

Do-Over Day Two

The day before, I'd felt like I was walking the red carpet. Now I felt like I was walking the plank.

It seemed like everyone's eyes were boring into me when I got to school. It wasn't my imagination. Lips curled. Tongues *tsk*ed. Eyes rolled. "Show-off," I heard someone mutter. "Egghead," another voice said.

So much for my Instant Popularity Plan. I didn't get it. It had worked for Mom. I sighed. Maybe Mom wasn't as brilliant in everyone else's eyes as she was in Grandma's. Or maybe she didn't club people over the head with her intelligence the way I had. Whatever. At least Darcy and her clique still liked me better than they had before. In fact, they were waiting for me by my locker.

"Elsa!" Darcy spat out in a loud whisper as I approached them. "I need to see your social studies homework!"

"My what?" I asked.

"Your *social studies homework!*"

I guess my hesitation took her off guard, because she softened her approach. "It's not like I'm going to copy or anything," she explained, looking earnest. "It's just that I had cheerleading practice last night and had to rush through my homework. I thought if I could borrow *yours* for a few minutes, I could . . . you know . . . double-check my work."

Martin was passing us in the hall. He gave me a knowing look. His words rang in my ears: *"Intelligence doesn't carry much weight with Darcy and her clique, unless they're trying to use you."*

Darcy's attitude suddenly changed again. She was getting impatient. "We're friends, right?" she demanded, planting her hands on her hips.

Hmmmm. Good question.

"Elsa!" she barked. "Friends help each other out."

I opened my locker and fished around for a couple of books. I turned and calmly replied, "Find me a friend and I'll help her."

Darcy's mouth dropped open.

I grinned. I could do better than that. I rubbed my locket. "Do-over," I said.

Ten-second rewind.

"Friends help each other out," Darcy repeated.

"What kind of a friend are you, Darcy?" I said. "You're snotty and mean and fake. You're just using me! I'd rather have *no* friends than have *you* as a friend."

The clique, stunned, looked at Darcy, whose almond-shaped eyes were narrowing into slits.

Nah. Couldn't risk it. I sighed. "Do-over."

Ten-second rewind.

"Friends help each other out," Darcy repeated.

I rolled my eyes. I had my hands full today undoing my disastrous reputation as a brainiac; I'd have to deal with Darcy later.

"Can we deal with this later?" I said. "We're going to be late for Mr. Wright's class."

Darcy looked dissatisfied but followed me along with the others to Mr. Wright's class. My mind swam as I tried to plot my next move. I wanted to undo the damage I'd done the day before without driving Darcy and her friends away. I know, I know . . . with friends like that, who needs enemies? But I figured it took a few phony friendships to get the ball rolling toward being popular. I'd have to think of some new way to impress Darcy and her clique. But right now, I had some serious dumbing down to do.

❧

"So," Mr. Wright said, clapping his hands together. "Tell me what you think of Scout and Jem." He was referring to the main characters from *To Kill a Mockingbird*. Our homework was to read the first four chapters.

Which I did.

Which no one would ever know.

Because no matter *what* I thought about *To Kill a Mockingbird* (which I was actually enjoying), I was keeping my mouth shut.

"Anyone?" Mr. Wright asked. Silence. His eyes zeroed in on me. "Elsa?"

I gave an apologetic shrug.

He looked puzzled but quickly moved on. "Darcy?" he said.

"Huh?" said Darcy, who hadn't been paying attention.

Mr. Wright cleared his throat. "Jem and Scout. What do you think about Jem and Scout?"

Darcy looked bored. "They're fine," she replied.

Mr. Wright folded his arms. "Could you be a little more specific?"

Darcy tossed her mane of hair over her shoulder. "Um . . . they're . . . you know . . . they're nice. Just a couple of regular guys."

Martin snickered. "Except that one of them is a girl," he muttered.

Darcy flashed him a cutting look. "Uh, *duh*," she said. "People say 'guys' to mean 'girls,' too."

"Right you are," Martin shot back. "How silly of me to think you might not have a clue what you're talking about."

Darcy and her clique rolled their eyes, but I couldn't help laughing.

Well . . . maybe I *could* help it. As soon as I did, the clique flashed furious glares at me.

I rubbed my locket.

"Do-over."

Ten-second rewind.

"Right you are," Martin repeated. "How silly of me

to think you might not have a clue what you're talking about."

I rolled my eyes dramatically, along with the rest of the cool kids.

Better.

"Okay, now that we've established their genders . . ." Mr. Wright was saying, "Elsa, what can you tell us about Scout and Jem? If they moved next door to you, what would you tell your friends about them?"

I glanced up quickly, like I hadn't been paying attention. "Sir?" I asked, sounding bored.

Mr. Wright looked puzzled. Then annoyed. "Share something with us about the main characters," he said evenly.

"Oh." I waved a hand through the air. "They're cute, I guess."

Giggles rippled through the classroom. I gulped, feeling relieved by the students' approval but bothered by Mr. Wright's expression.

"*Cute?*" Mr. Wright repeated. "You think they're *cute?* This brilliant critique from the same student who pondered the novel's universality in class yesterday?"

I yawned dramatically. "Sorry, Mr. Wright, but this novel isn't exactly a thrill ride, if you know what I mean." Nice touch. Sounded like something Darcy would say.

Mr. Wright's eyes narrowed. "Yesterday, you said it was one of your favorite books," he said, coming closer, the better to see me with his big brown eyes.

"What*ever*," I said. "Hey, if you like it, I like it. In fact, it's my very favorite book of all time, the most awesome book ever. Is that better?" My voice dripped with sarcasm.

The kids tittered in appreciation, which should have made me happy.

But all I could focus on was Mr. Wright's look of disap-pointment.

TWELVE

"Psssst! Elsa! Bathroom!"

Gathering my books as the bell rang, I glanced up at the sound of Darcy's hissing (she would have been more subtle if she'd shouted). Thank heaven Mr. Wright's class was finally over. My new-and-improved moron act left me feeling drained.

Darcy strode toward the bathroom with Jade and Carter skittering in her wake.

"What?" I asked when I joined them in the bathroom.

"Social studies homework," Darcy snapped. "I need it. Now!"

Shall I curtsy when I present it to you, Your Majesty?

"Hey, Elsa," Jade piped up. "Why were you suddenly brain-dead in Mr. Wright's class? What happened to Miss Know-It-All?"

I rolled my eyes. "If Mr. Wright's class was any more

boring, it would be on the Discovery Channel," I said, trying to ignore the dull ache in the pit of my stomach.

"But I thought you loved that stuff," Jade persisted.

I winked. "I just wanted to impress the teacher. I'm over it now."

Darcy seemed to have forgotten why she'd summoned me to the bathroom. She was perched on the counter by the mirror, smudging something shimmery and pastel-colored on her eyelids.

She glanced at me and curled her lip. "Wanna borrow some makeup?" she asked.

"Yeah, Elsa," Jade coaxed. "You could be . . . you know . . . kinda cute . . . if you just *did* something with yourself."

Carter and Darcy nodded. "It's not that she's a dog or anything," Darcy murmured as if I wasn't in the room. "It's just . . ." She turned from the mirror long enough to study me from head to toe, then raised a single eyebrow and slowly shook her head.

Jade and Carter *mmmm*'d in agreement.

"Here." Darcy had turned back to the mirror and was holding an arm straight out in my general direction. I looked at the plastic container with a dozen gooey colors of eye shadow.

I'd never worn makeup before—Dad would freak—but what the heck.

I squeezed next to Darcy in front of the mirror, though she didn't budge an inch for me, and began dabbing pale pink shadow over my eyes.

"Eeeeewww!" Darcy moaned. "That color is seriously atrocious on you."

The clique cackled.

I rubbed my locket.

"Do-over."

Ten-second rewind—just enough time for the pink stuff to disappear from my eyes.

Darcy handed me the makeup again. This time, when I joined her at the mirror, I gave her a little hip shove. "Some room, please?" I said, trying to sound annoyed and casual at the same time. Darcy cut her eyes at me, but she moved. The other girls looked impressed.

I smeared on some mauve eye shadow. Definitely more mature. I hoped.

"Gah-ross!" Darcy moaned.

What now?

"That color is seriously tacky on you, Elsa," she said. "Have you ever heard of a concept called taste? It's definitely underrated."

Jade and Carter giggled.

I sighed and rubbed my locket. "Do-over."

I opted for a grayish color.

Darcy sized me up, then wailed, "Yuck! I don't think so."

I put my hands on my hips. "What color do you suggest, Darcy?" I said.

"Try the green. It'll pick up the flecks in your eyes," she said, still staring at herself.

I rubbed my locket.

"Do-over."

Gone was the gray. I went for the green. Now would she be satisfied?

"Gag!" Darcy said as she checked out my latest choice (the one she had no recollection of just recommending), pushing a finger into her open mouth.

I huffed in exasperation. Was there any pleasing her?

Jen came running into the bathroom.

"You'll never believe what I just heard!" she gasped.

Darcy kept applying makeup. "What?" she asked in a bored voice.

"I overheard Charlotte Channing say she has a crush on Eric! Darcy's Eric! She's going to invite him to the spring dance!"

That got Darcy's attention big-time. She spun around.

Hmmmm . . . gossip. Of course. That was what this crowd really valued.

I rubbed my locket.

"Do-over!"

Ten-second rewind.

Jen came running into the bathroom.

"You'll never believe what I just heard!" she gasped.

"You mean about Charlotte?" I said, sounding bored.

Jen looked stunned. "You know?"

"About her crush on Eric?" I shrugged. "Sure. She's going to invite him to the spring dance."

Darcy slapped a hairbrush angrily against the sink.

"I don't think so!" she sputtered, tossing her makeup into her purse. "I think it's time for a little heart-to-heart with Shabby Charlotte." She jutted her chin into the air and left.

Jade, Jen and Carter were staring at me. "How did you

know about Charlotte?" Jen asked. "When I was eavesdropping, she was swearing her best friend to secrecy, saying she was the only one who knew."

"It's a little obvious, don't you think?" I said, and the girls nodded as if yes, it had been obvious all along. "Plus, I just pick up on things."

"Elsa," Jade said, leaning in closer, "come with us when we go to the mall."

"And sit with us at lunch today!" Carter chimed in. "I'll give you some makeup tips."

I smiled. Yep. Gossip was definitely worth its weight in gold with this group.

$$\bullet$$

Carter whipped out her makeup bag at lunch as we scooted our chairs around the table.

"I told Elsa I'd give her some makeup tips," she said to Darcy. Jade and Jen nodded.

Darcy spun in her seat to face Carter, dropping her jaw in astonishment. "You?" she sneered at Carter. "Girlfriend, I've got news for you: You need some serious fashion instruction before you can even *think* of giving tips to poor Elsa."

Carter blushed and stared down at her makeup. She looked like her ego had just been flattened by a truck.

"I think Carter always looks really pretty," I said. Jen, Jade and Darcy rolled their eyes and gave each other knowing looks.

Do-over? Nah. . . .

"First of all," Darcy intoned, "Carter's idea of great

fashion is to totally copy me." She gave Carter a sympathetic smile, but Carter was still staring at her makeup. "Which would be okay, Carter, except that your coloring is, like, totally different."

"Right, Carter," Jade piped up. "Darcy is blond and tan, and you're redheaded with pasty, ghost-white skin."

Carter looked ready to cry.

"It's porcelain skin," I said softly. "Your skin is beautiful." Carter gave me a trace of a smile.

Darcy huffed. "Hel-*lo*, 4-1-1. When you put pink lipstick on ghost-white skin, you look like a peppermint stick." Jade and Jen laughed on cue.

"You gave me that lipstick for my birthday, Darcy," Carter said, her voice trembling.

"Duh! So I could borrow it!"

She laughed heartily; then Jade and Jen joined in. My blood was boiling as Carter sank deeper into her chair.

"Carter," Darcy explained, "we all know you're wearing more makeup to try to get Brian to notice you"—Carter gasped—"which is fine, except number one, use the right colors for your ghost-white complexion, and number two, you know Brian likes Jade."

Now Carter's tears spilled onto her cheeks. "You promised not to tell, Darcy!" she whispered.

"Everybody already knows you like Brian," Jade purred. "It's, like, so obvious. I don't even care, because he's so not my type. Still, that doesn't mean you'll make him like you by walking around looking like a peppermint stick."

Enough!

"Shut up!" I sputtered. "How can you call yourself

Carter's friends when you're being so mean to her? Maybe you're all just jealous of her skin."

Dead silence. Even Carter was sliding away.

Darcy's look chilled me. "Fine, Sludge," she said in a clipped tone. "You're right. We're terrible friends. So why are you hanging with us? There's your boyfriend, Martin. There are plenty of seats around him."

I rolled my eyes and rubbed my locket.

"Do-over."

I had no choice. Did I?

Ten-second rewind. "Still, that doesn't mean you can make him like you by walking around looking like a peppermint stick," Jade said to Carter.

I cleared my throat loudly. "Hey, you guys!" I said cheerfully. "We're talking about *my* makeover, remember? I've never used makeup before. Help me with my colors."

Mission accomplished. Carter still looked miserable, but now all eyes were on me.

Darcy fell into stride. "Well," she said knowingly, "you're a fall. You know . . . your season." She sized me up with expert eyes. "Light brown hair, green eyes . . . think pink tones."

So now she likes me in pink? I groaned to myself.

Darcy grabbed Carter's makeup bag and browsed through it. She pulled out some blush and began dusting it on my cheeks. Sitting back to survey her work, she frowned. "You need to get some sun, Elsa," she said.

"Hel-*lo*," I said playfully. "Ya ever hear of skin cancer?"

Darcy pursed her lips. "Uh, we're, like, teenagers," she said, and the others nodded. Darcy continued putting more stuff on my face. "Elsa, your hair is ultra-stringy. It's like yarn or something," she said, fussing over me like I was a doll. "No offense. But you're obviously using some brand X shampoo. You gotta use the expensive stuff. And what's with the tacky necklace?"

My heart skipped a beat. "Oh . . . just a family heirloom." I slipped the locket under my blouse and made a mental note to keep it under my shirt from then on.

"And your nails!" Jade piped in. "Have you ever heard of a nail file?"

"I've got one in my makeup bag," Carter volunteered, cheerful now that she was off the hot seat.

"And the eyebrows!" Jen said. The clique nodded, enjoying their expertise as they tackled Project Elsa. "It looks like two caterpillars are crawling across your forehead," Jen said. "No offense."

"We have got to get Elsa to a cosmetic counter . . . fast," Darcy said. "Hmmmm . . . I'll be in L.A. with my dad this weekend. But next Saturday, the mall. Bring your dad's credit card," she told me. "And in the meantime . . . don't wear green. It clashes with your eyes."

I know what you're thinking. What's in it for me, to surrender myself to Darcy and her clique and let them mold me to their taste? Was that Mom's voice in my head that I heard *tsk-tsk*ing?

Lighten up, I said to the voice. *It's just makeup. And the girls are being nice to me . . . kinda.* It was fun feeling popular.

Forgoing the color green seemed like a small price to pay.

THIRTEEN

LaniAck: Where R U?

I logged on to my computer as soon as I got home from school. Lani was waiting, anxious to know all the latest news from Horror Springs Middle School.

I longed to tell her about the past couple of days. My do-over power was so overwhelming, I could hardly believe it. It would feel so great to tell my best friend. But I couldn't.

DolfinGrl: I'm rite here.

My screen name wasn't particularly inventive . . . just a nod to my love of dolphins. Mom used to cringe when she saw my IM spelling. "Chill, Mom," I'd say. "I'm talking to Lani, not writing my college thesis."

LaniAck: Wassup?

DolfinGrl: Just chillin. How are the Slice Girls?

LaniAck: 1 of them broke a nail today and called 911.

DolfinGrl: Fashion emergency! Hey, U won't believe this: Some girls gave me makeup tips at lunch 2day. They're taking me to the mall next weekend to help me buy supplies.

LaniAck: Get out! R U turning into a Slice Girl?

DolfinGrl: Not in this lifetime. But they're being nice to me . . . kinda. Your advice is working.

LaniAck: So you dumped the nerd?

DolfinGrl: Martin's not a nerd. He's nice and smart and funny.

LaniAck: You've just defined the word nerd, nerd. Now, quit being so nerdy.

DolfinGrl: I'm trying!

I paused.

DolfinGrl: Lani, I have major news to tell you.

I couldn't keep this a secret.

Suddenly, LaniAck was logged off her computer. My phone rang.

"Hello?" I answered.

"What's your major news?" Lani sounded breathless.

"I'd rather tell you in person, Lani. It's pretty . . . unbelievable."

Lani squealed so loudly, I had to pull the phone away from my ear. "Tell me now!" she shrieked.

I took a deep breath.

The words tumbled out. "My mom came to see me a couple of nights ago . . . she was right there on my bed . . . and she said that for the next month, whenever something happens that I don't like, I can say 'Do-over' and the whole world rewinds ten seconds so I can do it over again."

Silence.

Total silence.

Finally, Lani spoke. "I'm getting my mom," she said slowly.

"Do-over!"

Ten-second rewind. "Tell me now!" she shrieked.

Whew. That was close. No matter how much I was dying to tell this secret, I had to keep my mouth shut. What good would it do me to have Lani . . . and her mother, of all people . . . thinking I was nuts?

"ELSA!" Lani screeched, making me jump as I held the phone. "What is your major news?"

Hmmm . . . what could I tell her? Oh, right. . . . "I'm entering an essay contest at school."

Lani groaned. "That's major?" she said.

Sorry, Lani. It's the best I can come up with on a moment's notice. "The winner gets a laptop," I said.

Lani groaned. My major news would have to suffice. "So what's the topic?" she finally asked.

" 'What I've Learned in Seventh Grade.' Pretty lame, huh?"

"Totally. What are you going to write about? The secret ingredients in mystery meat?"

I smiled. "I dunno. My language arts teacher wants us to

make it fresh and original. I don't have much homework. Maybe I'll start working on it today."

"Let me read it when you're through," Lani said. "And next time you have major news to share, give me plenty of notice so I can alert the media."

I laughed. "Gotta go, Lani," I said. "Someone's ringing our doorbell. I'll call you soon."

I hung up the phone and went to the door.

It was Martin.

"Martin . . ."

"I didn't finish planting your grandmother's pansies yesterday. I told her I'd be back this afternoon. Snowball was clawing at the front door, so . . . here she is."

Grandma's cat tumbled from his arms and scampered down the hall.

"Martin, is that you?" Grandma called, coming to the door.

"Hi, Mrs. Jameson," he said. "I was just letting Snowball in the house before I got started in the backyard."

"Thanks, dear. Stop in when you want a cold drink and help yourself. You know the drill."

"Okay," he responded. "But I'll only be here a few minutes. I have a baseball game later."

"Yes, baseball!" Grandma said. "How's your team doing?"

"Not bad," Martin said. "My contribution is to stay off the field. But I've got a great view from the dugout."

"Oh, you're being silly," Grandma said, putting her hand on his cheek. "I'm sure you're a very valuable member of the team."

Martin lowered his head, smiling at the floor. "Whatever you say."

"Have you met my granddaughter, Elsa?" Grandma said.

"We've met," I said. "We have all the same classes."

"Oh, wonderful! Martin's such a bright young man. You'll have lots in common."

Martin shot me a knowing glance.

"I'll be doing laundry," Grandma said. "Holler if you need anything."

She walked off, leaving me face to face with Martin.

"A lot in common," Martin said dryly.

"Is that a bad thing?" I asked.

"It's a bogus thing," he responded. "We have nothing in common."

"That's not true. We both like books and writing."

"I'm not sure what you like," Martin said, "but whatever it is, I'm sure you have to run the list past Darcy for permission to like it."

I sighed and rubbed a sweaty palm against the doorknob.

"I'm just trying to make friends and fit in," I murmured.

Martin shook his head slowly. "It's one thing to fit in, Elsa. It's another to give in."

I fiddled with the knob. "What's that supposed to mean?"

"You're not like them," Martin said. "At least I think you're not. Or I thought you weren't."

My face flushed. "Why is it so terrible to want some friends? And why can't you give Darcy and her friends a chance? Do you even know them?"

Martin rolled his eyes. "What's to know?" he said.

"They're total snobs whose idea of intellectual stimulation is to color-coordinate their shoes with their nail polish."

I studied him silently for a moment. "Maybe you're the snob," I finally said. "And by the way, why are you on the baseball team if you hate it so much?"

Martin narrowed his eyes and stared at his feet. "My mom makes me."

"Because she wants you to fit in, maybe?" I asked defensively.

"Glad you've got it all figured out," he said, shooting me an icy glare. "I'm gonna go hang out with some weeds. Bye, Elsa. Enjoy your new friends."

❂

ROUGH DRAFT #1

What I've Learned in Seventh Grade
By Elsa Alden

When my mom was still alive, she and my dad went on a couple of trips to foreign countries as volunteers for an organization dedicated to ridding the world of land mines. They told me about kids who had lost arms and legs because they made the mistake of playing tag in a field that had explosives buried from some stupid, long-forgotten war. One wrong move and blam! The kids were either killed or marred for life. The kids who managed to escape the land mines soon caught on that although the fields looked safe, they really weren't. They started tiptoeing through their lives. Eventually, they stopped going out into the fields altogether.

I don't mean to make light of what happened to them, but sometimes I feel like middle school is filled with hidden land mines. In elementary school, I was like the carefree little kids, going wherever I wanted, acting however I wanted. But once I started middle school, I stepped on a couple of land mines . . . wearing pants to school that were just a tad too short, or piping up in science class before I learned that it wasn't cool . . . and I started tiptoeing. That's what I'm doing now, especially since I'm in a brand-new school and am really clueless about where the explosives are buried.

It's not so bad watching every step I take. A little tiring, yes, and I'd rather go skipping through the daisies like I used to, or even tromping on them if I feel like it. But I can't do that anymore. I'm learning if you make a few key friends, you get a better feel for where the explosives are buried, and you're less likely to blow yourself up. I think that's the trick. Stay quiet, lie low and find some friends who can tip you off, or at least soften the blow if you misstep. If the friends seem a little mean and snobby at first, well, maybe it's because they learned the rules of the game earlier than the other kids, and they've gotten smarter at playing it. I'm trying to learn to play the game their way.

I reread what I'd written, then frowned and hit the Delete key. It didn't feel right. Nothing felt right these days.

✪

"Your mom and I used to love to sit outside, watching the stars."

As Dad and I sat on Grandma's front porch swing that evening, he squeezed me tightly to his side with one arm and pointed to the sky with the other. "We sat on this very swing when we were dating," he said. "You see, I was too cheap to take Mom out."

I giggled. "So it's not that the stars were romantic . . . it's just that they were free," I said.

"Hey, don't knock it."

We sat silently for a few minutes, looking up at the sky and listening to the lazy creak of the swing as it slowly moved back and forth.

"So, Elsa," Dad finally said, his eyes on the stars, "is your new principal still ready to enroll you at Harvard?"

I smiled. "After today, he may think kindergarten is a better fit."

The swing creaked. "Really, honey. How's it going?" Dad asked. "Do you like your new school?"

I was silent for a minute, thinking about my answer. "It's okay," I finally said.

"Really?"

I shrugged. "Really. My language arts teacher is pretty cool. The lunch food is tolerable, in a disgusting sort of way.

And since you threatened to make me skip a grade, I spent the day taking power naps in class."

I laughed at Dad's worried expression. "Don't worry," I assured him. "Your obnoxious 'My kid is an honor student' bumper sticker is secure."

Dad nodded. "It is pretty obnoxious. I was thinking about getting a new one to put over it that says, 'My honor student's dad likes to brag.' "

Creak. Creak. I loved the sound of Grandma's swing.

"How about friends?" Dad asked.

I shrugged again, gazing down at my hands.

Dad held his foot firmly on the porch, stopping the swing. "Elsa?" he said, looking concerned. "You can talk to me, honey. Have you made new friends? Are you lonely?"

Suddenly, my eyes brimmed with tears. "I think I'll be lonely for the rest of my life without Mom," I said softly. "And I'm not sure anymore what it means to be a friend. If you're nice enough to snotty girls so that at least they say mean things to your face rather than behind your back, is that friendship?"

I glanced at Dad and was devastated to see that his own eyes were glistening with tears. Oh no. I could bear just about anything but making Dad sad. Making Dad sadder.

I quickly rubbed my locket. "Do-over!"

Ten-second rewind. "You can talk to me, honey," Dad said. "Have you made new friends? Are you lonely?"

I gave him a warm smile. "I'm fine, Dad. Everything's going great. Really. I'm going to the mall next weekend with some girls. They're gonna help me buy some makeup." Dad looked a little wary. "That *is* okay, isn't it?" I asked him.

He shrugged. "Sure. You seem a little young for makeup to me, but what do I know? I mean, it's not like I'm an honor student at Harbin Springs Middle School."

I smiled, and he smiled back.

"The trip to the mall sounds like fun," he said. "I'll even give you a lift. I'm anxious to meet your new friends."

✿

I begged my mom for another visit when I got in bed that night.

"Can you come back for just a little while?" I whispered, gazing up at the plastic stars on my ceiling, which glowed brightly now that the room was dark.

Nothing.

"Where are you, Mom? Are you blending in?"

Silence.

"I need you," I groused, still whispering to the ceiling. "How do I know if I'm using my do-overs right unless you give me some feedback?"

Still nothing.

"You told me to use them wisely, Mom," I said, still gazing at my stars. "So how am I doing? I think I'm finally figuring out the rules of this middle school . . . and that's a good thing, right?"

Silence.

Frustrated, I rolled onto my side and closed my eyes.

Maybe my mom would give me some advice in a dream. As I drifted to sleep, I remembered her words: *"Use your do-overs wisely. The only person you can change is yourself. Be true to yourself, Elsa. That's all I ask."*

Be true to yourself, Elsa.

FOURTEEN

Do-Over Day Five

My first do-over the next week happened before the morning bell had rung. I was at my locker grabbing my language arts book when Martin came walking down the hall. As usual, his nose was in a book. Suddenly, he walked straight into an open locker door, knocking himself off balance and falling on his back. All the kids in the hall laughed. He blushed as he felt around for his glasses, put them back on and got up.

I rubbed my locket.

"Do-over."

Ten-second rewind. As Martin started walking down the hall toward the open locker door, I ran over and slammed it shut . . . much to the surprise of the guy who was rifling through it for his books.

"OW!" the guy screamed, yanking his thumb from the

slammed locker. "You just shut the locker on my thumb, moron! What were you thinking?"

Uh-oh. The law of unintended consequences.

"My bad," I muttered, rubbing my locket. "Do-over."

Ten-second rewind. As Martin started walking down the hall toward the open locker door, I ran toward him, positioning myself between him and the locker. With his nose still buried in his book, this time he ran into me rather than the locker door, and knocked me to the floor.

Now everybody was laughing at *me*.

Everybody but Martin.

He stopped abruptly and stared down at me, looking concerned.

"Sorry," he said gently, extending his hand to help me up. "I wasn't watching where I was going. Are you okay?"

"Yeah," I said, brushing myself off as I rose to my feet.

"Watch where you're going, idiot!" someone grumbled at Martin. It was Carter, coming to collect her own books.

Do-over? Nah. I didn't have time to undo the fall. Why hadn't I just left well enough alone?

"He is such a dweeb!" Carter moaned as Martin walked away, glancing quickly at me over his shoulder.

"It was an accident," I said. "Actually, it was my fault. I stepped in his way."

Carter grinned mischievously. "Hey . . . I'm beginning to think you really are in love with him."

I rolled my eyes. "No, Carter. I am not in love with him," I said, accentuating each word. "I've known him for a week. I'm just clumsy. Got it?"

She shrugged as she retrieved her books. Maybe this was a good time to sympathize with her about the way the girls had treated her in the lunchroom.

"Hey, Carter . . . ," I said, trying to sound casual. "Those things Darcy and the others were saying Friday in the lunchroom . . . you know, about your lipstick and your coloring, or whatever . . ."

Carter blushed. "What about it?" she asked, suddenly defensive.

"Nothing," I said quickly. "I just think you do a good job with your makeup. You always look really cute." I paused. "I hope they didn't upset you."

Carter's mouth dropped open and she spun around to face me. "They're, like, totally my friends, Elsa!" she said, then glanced nervously around the hallway. "Friends tell each other when they're making fools of themselves. Darcy did me a favor." She leaned close to me, as if to tell me a secret. "I threw that pink lipstick in the trash can as soon as lunch was over," she whispered.

She shut the locker door.

"But if you like the lipstick, who cares what they think?" I persisted.

She gazed down at her feet. "Sometimes I just get stuff wrong, okay?" she said quietly.

Carter wasn't evil. She was just desperate for Darcy's friendship. I wondered what Carter was really like under all the superficial stuff.

❧

As we walked into Mr. Wright's class, I reminded myself of my new secret identity: Knower of All Gossip. I had to be careful; I didn't want to embarrass anyone or hurt their feelings. But as long as someone was going to spill the beans, it might as well be me.

"How was L.A.?" Jade asked Darcy as they walked into class.

"Totally awesome," Darcy cooed. "The hot movie star and I had a milk shake together during a break in taping. Of course, Dad would never let anything come of it because of our age difference, but I think he is seriously crushing on me."

Jade gasped. "Please tell us who he is, Darcy. Please?"

Darcy flung a manicured hand through the air. "I don't go blabbing our business. God. You are so immature."

Jade blushed, then said, "Well, I don't have any news *that* exciting, but I did hear that Jen barfed in dance class yesterday, all over the teacher's shoes."

Hmmmm. I rubbed my locket.

"Do-over."

Ten-second rewind.

"Of course, Dad would never let anything come of it because of our age difference," Darcy repeated, "but I think he is seriously crushing on me."

I elbowed my way in between the two of them. "So did you hear about Jen's barf fest yesterday in dance class?" I said. "Totally gross. And right on the teacher's shoes!"

Jade did a double take. "How did you know?" she asked. "You're not in her dance class."

I shrugged casually. "It's no biggie. I just hear things . . . ya know?"

Darcy glanced across the room at Jen with a sneaky smile.

"I am gonna seriously rag on her about this," she said. "But first, I'm gonna ask where she got those new shoes. She totally copies me. I saw those in *Cosmo Girl* last week and told her how much I liked them. I guess she looked all over town trying to find them when she realized they were cool."

I rubbed my locket. "Do-over."

Ten-second rewind.

"I am gonna seriously rag on her about this," Darcy repeated.

"Hey," I said, "look at Jen's shoes. I saw them in *Cosmo Girl* last week and thought about getting a pair, but they're way too young for me. I mean, they're fine for *her*. . . ."

Darcy sneered. "Totally babyish," she agreed.

As we walked toward Jen, Darcy suddenly clutched her stomach and began to make gagging noises.

"I think . . . I think . . . I think I'm gonna be sick," she moaned, then pretended to barf on Jen's new shoes. Jen looked too startled to respond.

"Elsa told us all about your barf fest," Darcy said coolly as Jade stifled a giggle. "Actually, I'd be doing you a favor to barf all over your hideous new shoes."

Jen blushed, managing a weak smile to keep from looking "too sensitive" (a favorite put-down of Darcy's), but she couldn't hide the hurt in her expression. Her eyes locked with mine for just a second, but I quickly looked away. Suddenly, I felt like I was about to barf myself.

But before I had too much time to dwell on it, I realized that Charlotte Channing had walked up to my desk.

"Thanks for blabbing all over school that I like Eric," she said with a steely expression.

I gulped. *But I didn't blab it all over school,* I wanted to say. *I only blabbed it to a few girls in the bathroom. And if I hadn't, Jen would have. Besides, what's the big deal?*

But Charlotte walked away before I had a chance to blurt out the thoughts that were bouncing around inside my head. Do-over? What was the point? How could I convince Charlotte that I hadn't done anything wrong when I didn't even believe it myself?

"All right, class, let's get seated," Mr. Wright said.

I breathed a sigh of relief. Finally, I could concentrate on language arts rather than shoes, or barfing, or who liked who, which I really didn't care about anyway. . . . Except that I couldn't get too comfortable. I made a mental note that I had to keep up my brain-dead routine. I had nothing to show for the Albert Einstein impersonation except for a school full of glares and the threat of skipping eighth grade. Couldn't risk that.

"Let's open *To Kill a Mockingbird* to chapter nine," Mr. Wright was saying. "Elsa, what are you learning about Scout's relationship with Atticus as the book progresses?"

"Uh . . ." Actually, I was learning that her father's opinion was the most important thing to Scout in the whole world because her father was a good person who cared only about doing the right thing and couldn't care less whether anybody liked it or not.

That's what I thought. But it isn't what I said.

"Uh . . . ," I repeated. "Sorry, Mr. Wright. Can you repeat the question?"

I managed to sound super-uninterested, which made Darcy snicker in appreciation. But it was Mr. Wright's reaction that I noticed. He looked like he was giving up on me.

My heart sank. (If my heart had sunk any further that morning, it would have been in my shoes.) Maybe I could be just a little bit smart, just *kind of* my actual self? But I wouldn't get the chance . . . not that day, anyway. Mr. Wright didn't call on me again a single time . . . until the bell rang.

"Elsa, I'd like to see you after class," he said as everyone started gathering up their books.

Uh-oh. That wasn't good. I took a deep breath and walked up to his desk.

"Yes, Mr. Wright?"

He tapped his pencil on his desk as if he was trying to decide what to say next. He looked me in the eye. I pulled my book tighter against my chest.

"How's it going, Elsa?" he asked, trying to sound casual. "How do you like your new school, your new town, your new . . . friends?"

Was this a trick question?

"Fine, Mr. Wright," I replied, sounding way too perky. "Everything's great."

He nodded. "You *are* going to submit an essay for the contest, aren't you?"

Another trick question?

I shrugged. "Sure . . . I guess. I mean, I haven't really given it much thought."

Mr. Wright grimaced slightly. "That's just it, Elsa. You're a thinker. Where is the thinker inside you hiding?"

I felt myself giving him a longing look. At that moment, what I wanted more than anything in the world was his approval, the approval of someone I genuinely liked and respected. I wanted him to like and respect me back. Fat chance. My eyes suddenly brimmed with tears. Could I really confide in him?

"I'm so confused, Mr. Wright," I blurted out, almost choking on the words as they tumbled rapid-fire out of my mouth. "I don't know how to act or what to say in this school." A tear rolled down my cheek. "I'm trying so hard to get people to like me, but what makes me feel really lonely is that nobody knows me."

Mr. Wright softened. He looked so kind and caring . . . and that was when I realized that Darcy and her clique, still making their way out of the classroom, had overheard what I said. They jabbed each other with their elbows and stifled giggles. "What*ever*, Elsa!" Darcy whispered.

My shoulders slumped and I rubbed my locket.

"Do-over."

Ten-second rewind.

"That's just it, Elsa," Mr. Wright said to me again. "You're a thinker. Where is the thinker inside you hiding?"

I scrunched my shoulders. "Ya got me, Mr. Wright," I said blandly. Darcy looked impressed as she brushed past. Whew. Much better.

Except that Mr. Wright looked disappointed. He tossed an annoyed glance at Darcy and Carter, then turned his gaze back to me.

"I was hoping you would contribute more in class, Elsa,"

he finally said. "I think you have a lot of interesting ideas and observations. I wish you would share them."

Right, Mr. Wright. I'll just draw lots of attention to myself, saying all kinds of smarmy brainiac things that seal my fate as a total loser, and then I'll have no friends, and everybody will be even snottier to me than they already are, and I'll be alone and miserable, but the good news is you'll be pleased that I'm sharing my interesting ideas and observations in class. Not.

But if Mr. Wright was so totally clueless, why did his opinion matter so much to me?

I shrugged and stared at my feet. "I guess I'm just trying to keep a low profile," I said softly, then looked up.

He nodded slowly, never shifting his gaze from my eyes. "Just don't lose yourself in the process. Okay?"

✿

"Sorry about our collision this morning." I glanced toward the sound of the voice. It was Martin, who had walked up to me in the lunch line as I took my tray.

I smiled. "Totally my fault," I said.

"No, it wasn't," he said. "True, you did seem to just kind of . . . appear . . . out of nowhere, but I wasn't watching where I was going. I really am sorry . . . and I'm sorry I ragged on you about your friends. Everybody's entitled to pick their own friends."

I smiled. "At this point, any friends would do."

He pursed his lips.

"Hey," I continued, "sorry Carter was so nasty to you this morning when I fell."

"She's always nasty," Martin said matter-of-factly.

I furrowed my brow. "She's just insecure, I think," I said, then leaned in closer. "She totally lets Darcy boss her around and cut her down. I don't get it."

"It's the price of admission," he stated flatly.

"Admission?"

"Admission to popularity," Martin said. "Too high a price, if you ask me." He looked at me quizzically. "How about you?"

I suddenly felt uncomfortable. "Meaning what? I'm not looking to be popular, thank you very much. I'm just looking to fit in."

Martin's expression turned pensive. "What if that's the same thing?"

I stared down at the ground . . . anywhere but at his probing eyes.

"Elsa! There you are!"

Carter was coming toward me. She grabbed my arm and led me to a lunch table where Darcy, Jade and Jen were sitting.

"Elsa, you have totally got to stop hanging around that dweeb," Darcy scolded as I sat down. "If you want to hang around us, that is. Otherwise, you're going to, like, pulverize our reputation."

"Right," I said under my breath, then quickly changed the subject. "Hey, that essay contest. Is anybody else entering?"

Darcy brightened at the topic. "Oh, right . . . the essay contest. Here's the thing, Elsa . . ."

She pursed her lips.

"Writing is not my thing," she explained, eliciting giggles from the other girls. "But you're really good at it . . . right?"

I shrugged. "I dunno . . . I'm okay, I guess."

"Right," Darcy said, nodding earnestly. "The thing is, I really hate it"—more giggles—"and I really could use some help on my essay."

My stomach tightened. "So you are entering?"

"Uh . . . duh!" she said, and the girls laughed on cue. "So, help me, Elsa, please? Won't you please help me with my essay?"

I decided to try to change the subject. "Hey, what's that hottie really like? Spill the dirt."

Darcy's expression turned dark. "Get over that, Elsa!" she snapped. "I told you, I have to be discreet about my dad's job." She lowered her voice and leaned closer. "It's especially important now. I think one of the tabloids spotted the hottie and me together last weekend, and our picture will probably be splashed all over the papers." She paused for effect. "Now, focus. Will you help me with my essay or not?"

I laughed. "As if," I said, mimicking their jargon. "I want to win that laptop for myself."

Darcy's jaw dropped. "How selfish!" she spat. "And after I offered to help you buy makeup!"

The other girls shot me icy glares.

Well . . . Darcy had a point. She did offer to help me buy makeup. Now that I thought about it, I realized I hadn't exactly asked her for help, but I guess that was beside the point. . . .

Here goes:

I rubbed my locket. "Do-over."

Ten-second rewind.

"Now, focus," Darcy repeated. "Will you help me with my essay or not?"

"Sure," I said quietly. "I'll help you."

FIFTEEN

Do-Over Day Ten

"Dad. You're not listening to your big-band CD."

"I'm not?"

"Please, Dad. My new friends aren't Benny Goodman fans. Go figure."

Dad smiled as he backed out of Grandma's driveway.

"Well," he said, "far be it from me to broaden their horizons. What do they want to listen to?"

"I think Top Forty is a safe bet," I said, ejecting his CD and punching buttons on the radio until a familiar pop tune started blaring from the speakers.

"So these friends of yours are the cutting-edge type, huh?" Dad said, cruising down the street past the blankets of pink and purple azaleas. He followed my directions and we pulled into Carter's driveway. He tooted the horn and out they streamed . . . Darcy, then Jade, then Jen, then Carter, wearing identical low-cut jeans and skimpy little tops that exposed their midriffs. Their hair was parted down the middle and ironed sleekly straight.

"Are they quadruplets?" Dad asked, and I wasn't sure if he was kidding.

They piled into the backseat. "Hi," I said, leaning around to face them. "Darcy, Jen, Jade, Carter . . . this is my dad."

"Your dad," Carter said with a little sneer. "Isn't driving your daughter to the mall a mom thing?"

I guess now was as good a time as any. "My mom died last year," I said, aiming for a neutral tone. The girls drew quick breaths.

"Bummer," Jade said, and the others murmured in agreement.

"Yeah . . . bummer," I said.

"You know, it just so happens that the mall is my favorite place to hang out," Dad teased, trying to lighten the mood. I groaned. *No jokes, Dad,* I said in my head, hoping he was picking up on my vibes. *Please?*

"You hang out at the mall?" Darcy asked.

"Oh, all the time," Dad said, finding his rhythm. "The scented-candle store is my favorite. I could spend all day in there, just sniffing away."

Darcy tossed sideways glances at the others. "O . . . *kay,*" she said.

"He's kidding," I explained. "Dad, can you save it for *Star Search?*"

"Your dad's gonna be on *Star Search?*" Carter asked, leaning forward.

Darcy rolled her eyes. "Carter," she scolded. "You are, like, so naïve. It was a joke."

"Oh." Carter settled back into her own seat. "So how did your mom die, Elsa?"

"Aneurysm," I replied, staring straight ahead.

"What's that?"

"A blood vessel burst in her brain."

"God!" Jen gasped. "I can't imagine my mom being dead, even though she's, like, so annoying."

"I wish I'd appreciated mine more when I had the chance," I said a little too sharply.

"Okay, everybody, this conversation is, like, totally bringing me down," Darcy said decisively. "Makeup. This trip is about makeup, remember?"

Right. Makeup.

"Elsa, your dad isn't gonna stay with us while we're shopping, is he?" Darcy asked, as if Dad was invisible.

"Oh, no," Dad volunteered cheerfully. "I'll be in the scented-candle store, sniffing away . . . remember?"

I shot him a stern glance and he shrugged apologetically.

"Not that we wouldn't enjoy having you around, Mr. Alden," Darcy said in a fake-sweet tone. "It's just that we have serious work to do on Elsa."

Dad looked a little nervous. "Don't work too hard," he said. "I kinda like her the way she is."

"Hey, did you hear about April Newsome?" Jade said. "Mrs. Stiffle caught her smoking under the basement stairs. April was so surprised, she stuck the cigarette in her ear and her hair caught on fire! I hear she's going to an alternative school."

The girls gasped in interest.

I rubbed my locket. "Do-over."

Ten-second rewind.

"Hey, did you hear about April Newsome?" Jade repeated.

"Oh, you mean about smoking under the basement stairs and catching her hair on fire when she tried to put the cigarette out in her ear?" I said casually. "I hear she's going to an alternative school."

Dad cast a little sideways glance at me, but I couldn't concern myself with that right now. The other girls had leaned closer to my seat.

"And I hear cigarettes aren't the only thing she's smoking," I said, turning toward them and raising an eyebrow.

"Elsa!" Dad barked.

"Sorry," I muttered. True, I was ad-libbing. But it was probably true (I didn't even know April Newsome, but if she was sticking cigarettes in her ear and setting her hair on fire, how bright could she be?), and it felt so good for the girls to be interested in what I was saying.

"Change the subject right now," Dad said through gritted teeth.

I twirled a piece of hair in my fingers. Was the clique's appreciation of my gossip worth my dad's disappointment in me? And was it worth the rumors that would be swirling all over school Monday about some girl I had never even met but who would hate me anyway as soon as she realized that the gossip could be traced back to me?

I was starting to wish I could do over my whole life.

The girls chatted while I looked out the window. I stared into the bright blue sky, trying to see the outline of the invisible moon and stars. No luck. *Mom?* I said in my head. *Ya there?*

Dad pulled into the mall parking lot. We piled out of the car. "Meet you in an hour at the food court," he called, and I turned around and waved.

Darcy, Jade, Jen, Carter and I were headed for the department store when we passed a little earring boutique. I decided to make a quick detour to cheer myself up.

"Hey, guys, let's check this place out," I said.

"Your ears aren't even pierced," Carter pointed out.

"Not yet . . . ," I said slyly.

The girls exchanged glances and giggled. "You're getting your ears pierced now?" Jade said. "Without even asking your dad?"

A lady on a stool behind the counter cleared her throat and asked if she could help us.

"How long would it take you to pierce my nose?" I asked.

The girls gasped. "Elsa!" Darcy said, but she sounded impressed.

"It doesn't take long at all," the woman responded.

"Less than ten seconds?" I persisted.

The lady raised a single eyebrow. "Am I being timed?"

"Kinda. . . . I can't do it unless it takes less than ten seconds."

The lady rose from her stool. "Let the countdown begin."

The girls looked on in astonishment as the lady rubbed alcohol on my nose, held a piercing gun against one nostril and zapped in a stud.

"Ooooowwww!" I howled.

But I took a second to check myself out in the mirror . . . and to check out the clique's jaws, which were practically hanging to the floor.

Okay. I'd had my fun. Now I knew what I looked like with a pierced nose.

I rubbed my locket. "Do-over."

Suddenly, my pierced nose was becoming unpierced. The pain immediately subsided and my nose was puncture-free.

"Let the countdown begin," the lady repeated, picking up where she had left off ten seconds before.

"Nah. Changed my mind."

The lady sneered at me as we breezed out of the store.

"Elsa, you are seriously whacked," Darcy murmured as we followed her to the department store.

She made a beeline to a makeup counter.

"May I help you?" the salesclerk said.

Darcy curled a lip. "No," she said briskly. "We'll be just fine on our own." She turned to me. "Elsa," she commanded, "you sit here."

I sat on a stool at the counter in front of a mirror that magnified my face ten times. My pores looked like moon craters. Darcy started fussing over the cosmetic samples. There were little rectangles filled with creams in various shades of red, ovals filled with blues, greens and grays and dozens of lipstick tubes. My mom had never worn much of this stuff, and I didn't know one goopy glob from another.

But Darcy did. She immediately started smearing things into my cheeks, then my eyelids, then my lips. Sometimes she'd rub off her handiwork and start over again, frowning into my face. I glanced into the mirror every once in a while, but all I could see was a larger-than-life nostril. Sometimes Jen, Jade or Carter would suggest something, but Darcy generally ignored them.

"Don't listen to them," she said, as if they weren't even there. "Jen and Jade are just now learning how to blend in their eye shadow, and Carter is hopeless."

Carter stared at the floor.

"No offense, Carter," Darcy chirped, "but redheads have to be very careful about their color choices. Especially your shade of red . . . that mousy, rust-colored red."

But no offense, I thought sarcastically, wishing just once that Carter would tell Darcy where to get off.

"And quit wearing white," Darcy told her sternly. "Really, that goes for all of you. It washes you out."

"But you wear white," Jen reminded her haltingly.

"Uh, duh. I'm tan." Darcy was rubbing something on my cheeks, moving her fingertips in a circular motion.

"What if we feel like wearing white?" I asked, squirming uncomfortably on my stool.

Darcy smirked. "Then I'll think you don't have enough sense to listen to good advice." She looked at the girls. "Wear white if you want to," she said with a saccharine-sweet smile. "I'll just have, like, a really bad cold that day and stay far, far away so I won't spread my germs."

The girls giggled.

This time, I couldn't hold my tongue. "Why are you laughing?" I asked them, totally frustrated. "She's insulting you."

The girls stiffened. "I'm teasing them, Elsa," Darcy said slowly. "Friends tease each other . . . unless they're so, like, uptight that they can't take it."

The clique nodded in agreement.

"Okay, Elsa," Darcy said sharply. "Time to pull out the credit card. And here's a shade of lipstick I just love, in case you want to treat your best friend to a little gift."

I was a pretty bright girl, right? So why was it taking me so long to catch on to the rules of this game?

◉

Dad did a double take when we met him in the food court.

"Elsa?" he said, peering at me like I was an outer-space alien.

"Hi, Dad," I said, managing a gooey Spicy Plum smile.

"How does she look, Mr. Alden?" Darcy asked.

Dad cleared his throat. "Colorful," he finally said. "Uh, girls, how about a bag of cookies on me?"

"Yum!" Carter replied, and they started walking toward the cookie stand. Dad gently took my arm.

"Elsa," he whispered in my ear, "what did she use to plaster that makeup on your face? A spatula?"

I smiled sheepishly. "A little over the top?" I asked.

"Not if you're juggling bowling pins at a birthday party with a bright red nose on your face. Otherwise . . ."

I nodded. "Don't worry, Dad. I'll wash it off when I get home."

He squeezed my hand. "It's just that you're so pretty the way you are. And you *are* only twelve, you know."

"Actually, I'm almost thirteen, Dad," I reminded him.

"So you like this stuff slathered all over your face?"

I sighed in frustration. "Yeah, I guess so," I muttered, staring down at my shoes.

Dad lowered his head until we were eye to eye. "Well, I don't think you need it. You've got so much going for you, honey. You're funny, smart, sensitive, sweet . . ."

I twirled my finger in the air. "Whoopee. Alert the media."

"The media may not be impressed," Dad said gently, "but I am. You know, last time we were at the mall, I couldn't drag you away from the dolphin posters. That's the Elsa I know."

My lips tightened. That Elsa was starting to seem like a distant memory.

Dad smiled. "Hey, one thing's for certain—your new friends sure do like cookies," he said, looking over at the cookie stand, where they were making their selections. "Let's go pay for them."

SIXTEEN

Darcy asked if she could stay at my house for a couple of hours after our mall trip. "We need to work on my essay," she said.

"We do?"

"Elsa, you promised!" she said indignantly.

"Okay, okay."

We settled into my bedroom, spilling pillows around the bed and propping our elbows on them.

"Now," Darcy said authoritatively, "here's what we'll do: I'll tell you what I want to include in my essay, and you take notes while I talk."

I rolled my eyes. "Why am I taking notes?"

"Uh, duh. I can't exactly talk and write at the same time."

She handed me a pad. "Here's what we need to include in my essay: cheerleader, dance squad—and the first person in the history of Harbin Springs Middle School to make the squad in the sixth grade—be sure to write that down. And of course we'll need to include all the pageants I've won, including this fall's swimsuit competition, where I was by far the skinniest girl in the contest—"

"Darcy," I interrupted, "Mr. Wright said we should avoid making a list of our activities."

She threw her hands in the air. "I can't exactly write about what I've learned in seventh grade if I don't include my most important accomplishments."

I rested my chin on my hand. "I think he wants us to go deeper than that," I said. "Sure, we learned about photosynthesis and percentages . . . but what have we learned about ourselves? About life? I think that's what the judges of the contest will be looking for."

Darcy examined her nails, looking bored. "Right," she said impatiently. "That's why you're here. I'll tell you about the important stuff I've learned and you can string the sentences together and make it sound good."

I caught her drift. "Then I would be writing your essay, Darcy," I said.

"Not writing it," Darcy protested. "Just making it sound better. I'm the one who did all that stuff, after all."

I guess I didn't look convinced.

"Look," she said, sitting up on the bed. "I put makeup on your face today, right? But it's still your face. I just made it pretty. All I'm asking you to do is return the favor. You take my life and put it on paper in pretty words." She paused, stiffening. "This *is* what we agreed to, after all."

Did we? I felt like burying my head under the covers, wishing Darcy and her pretty life would just disappear.

"I can't cheat," I groaned.

"I'm not asking you to cheat, Miss Perfect," Darcy said. "I'm asking you to help me. That's what friends do. They help each other."

"Well . . ." I took a deep breath. "I'll jot down a few notes and maybe come up with a rough draft. A very rough draft. Then you'll be on your own. Deal?"

"Right." Darcy smiled. "Oh, by the way, Elsa . . . did you bring your language arts notebook home?"

"Yes. . . ."

"Great. I left my worksheet at school. Let me borrow yours so I can write the questions down."

I didn't feel good about it, but . . . "Well . . . all right. But I've finished my homework, so write down the questions only, okay?"

She smiled. "Of course, silly."

Do-Over Day Twelve

"Darcy? Elsa? I'd like to see you both after class."

Omigod. It was only Monday morning, and the week was already looking shaky. Why would Mr. Wright want to see us after class? Darcy spun around in her seat to face me. She held up the palms of her hands. The other kids filed out of the classroom, and we went up to Mr. Wright's desk.

"Yes, sir?" I said nervously.

He glanced up from a pile of papers.

"Girls," he said. "I had a few moments to glance over your weekend homework assignment."

My heart sank to the pit of my stomach. What had Darcy written down when she borrowed my homework?

"Here's the thing," Mr. Wright said matter-of-factly. "Your answers were almost identical."

I felt my blood boiling. That Darcy! That . . . that snake!

Mr. Wright tapped a pencil on his desk. "I need an explanation."

Darcy waved a hand casually in the air. "I'm sure it's just a coincidence, Mr. Wright," she said sweetly. "Now, Elsa and I *did* discuss the book . . . I mean, she is new, and I've been trying to help her get settled. So maybe when I was explaining the book to her, I might have used some words and ideas that she ended up . . . you know . . . borrowing for her homework."

That skunk!

Mr. Wright shook his head.

"This is more than just a few similar ideas," he said, sounding sad. "One of you copied from the other." Pause. "And I'd like to know which one."

I clasped my sweaty palms together, wishing the floor would swallow me.

"Truly, Mr. Wright, I don't think anyone copied," Darcy said. "I mean, yes, when I was trying to help Elsa understand the story, she asked if she could glance at my homework, and I said okay, you know, trying to be a friend, but truly, I don't think she would have copied." She gazed at me. "Would you, Elsa?"

My mind raced. Do-over? But what would I do? What would I undo? I had spent the past few days trying to

convince Mr. Wright that I was an airhead. I guess I'd suc-
ceeded. I was too nervous to think straight.

"Did you cheat, Elsa?" Mr. Wright asked.

*No, Mr. Wright, I didn't. If I was desperate enough to need
Darcy's help understanding a book, I might as well quit school
right now. Darcy copied my homework. Isn't it obvious?*

But I had no proof. It was her word against mine, and
she gave her version first. Anything I said now would make
me look guilty.

I couldn't look him in the eye. "I don't cheat, Mr.
Wright. I don't know how this happened."

He cleared his throat. "Neither do I, Elsa, but unless you
have other information, I have no alternative but to con-
clude that cheating is exactly what happened. Did Darcy do
her homework first, then let you look at it?"

I shrugged, feeling like I was shrinking an inch a second.
Darcy stayed cool. "I guess I really don't know what happened," I whispered.

"Well, with only one version to choose from, I'll assume
Darcy's story is correct, and you get a zero on your homework, Elsa."

Tears brimmed in my eyes. I'd never had a zero in
my life.

Mr. Wright looked at me sternly. "If you need extra help
understanding an assignment, come to me. And it wouldn't
hurt to start paying attention in class." He paused. "That's
all."

I slunk out of the classroom. Betrayed.

"How could you do that to me?" I said, my voice trembling. Darcy tossed her hair over her shoulder.

"Oh, Elsa," she scoffed. "It's no biggie. Just one stupid homework grade. I thought my story was the best way to go because I was just sure he'd cut you some slack, you being new and all. Who knew he'd be so uptight?"

I was too humiliated to respond.

Then the thought popped into my head: *Use your do-overs wisely.* Finally, I was wising up. My do-overs could come in handier than I'd ever imagined. I had taken my share of hard knocks at Horror Springs Middle School. Now it was Darcy's turn.

✪

LaniAck: Where have U been? I haven't heard from you in days!

DolfinGrl: Sorry. I've been busy getting my nose pierced.

LaniAck: Very funny. How are the Harbin Springs Slice Girls doing?

DolfinGrl: Darcy copied my homework paper and told the teacher that I copied hers. He gave me a zero, which I think I'll stamp on my forehead to go with my nose ring. Thanks for that friendship advice, by the way.

LaniAck: Don't blame me! Why didn't you tell the teacher that Darcy's the one who cheated?

DolfinGrl: Long story. But I have a plan.

LaniAck: Tell, tell!

DolfinGrl: I'd tell you, but then I'd have to kill you. (LOL.) Let's just say that the most popular seventh grader at Horror Springs Middle School is about to take a little trip to the Land of the Losers.

LaniAck: TELL ME WHAT YOU'RE PLANNING!!! You're not going to get in trouble, R U?

DolfinGrl: That's the beauty of my plan. Risk-free to me, with maximum impact on Darcy. Can't give you any details, and I gotta log off . . . Dad's pounding on my door telling me to go to bed . . . but I have a secret weapon. TTYL.

I logged off and grinned, rubbing my locket. I could hardly wait for school to start the next day. That was when my secret weapon would begin taking direct aim at Darcy.

SEVENTEEN

Do-Over Day Thirteen

Part one of my plan was to pay close attention to Darcy's habits and routines. Oh, I wasn't obvious about it, and I was careful to keep being nice to Darcy and her clique. The more she trusted me, the more she would play into my hands. Revenge would be sweet . . . right?

My first Darcy Do-Over wasn't exactly the cleverest idea I'd ever had, but it was fun. After Mr. Wright's class, she slipped into the restroom to primp. I followed her in and watched her put a bottle of hair spray on the sink. After she brushed her hair, she reached for the hair spray without looking at it, then sprayed her hair.

I grinned and rubbed my locket. "Do-over."

Ten-second rewind. I glanced around the room quickly and saw a bottle of window cleaner. I swapped the window cleaner for the hair spray, then slipped out before Darcy could see me.

A few seconds later, I heard her yell, "Eeeeewww!"

She dashed out of the restroom. "I just sprayed window cleaner on my hair!" she shrieked.

I managed to look concerned as she tried to rub it out of her hair.

"I don't get it!" she wailed. "I know I put my hair spray on the sink right in front of me!"

"Streak-free," I murmured, inspecting the damage. She pouted, then flung her vinegar-scented hair over her shoulder and bolted down the hall.

As we settled into our next class, with Darcy combing her fingers through her sticky hair and our classmates sniffing curiously in her direction, I noticed that the odor seemed to aggravate Jen's allergies. She was sitting behind Darcy and barely had time to grab a tissue before she pitched her head forward with a hearty "Aaah-chooo!"

Perfect. *Thanks for the inspiration, Jen,* I thought as I rubbed my locket and murmured, "Do-over."

Just enough time to snatch Jen's tissue box and place it underneath her desk. "Aaaaah . . ." Jen's sneeze began and she grabbed for a tissue, which was no longer there. ". . . chooo!"

Darcy spun around to face her as Jen's eyes darted in search of her tissue box.

"You sneezed on my hair!" Darcy spat, at which point Jen found her tissues and began patting one against the back of Darcy's hair.

"Sorry . . . ," Jen said.

Darcy asked the teacher if she could be excused to tend to the collection of fluids accumulating in her hair. The teacher decided her fashion emergency didn't merit an extra trip to the restroom and told her to stay seated.

Darcy squirmed throughout the rest of class, then made a beeline for the restroom when the bell rang. Carter, Jade, Jen and I followed behind, the clique making *tsk*ing sounds about what a rough morning Darcy was having, although they were exchanging glances and trying not to grin.

"Girls," I said sternly. "Snot funny."

They covered their giggles.

Darcy was too busy fuming to notice. "I have window cleaner and snot in my hair," she snarled, grabbing a hairbrush from her purse. "I'll never use this brush again," she muttered.

Still, since she was using it now . . .

I rubbed my locket and said, "Do-over."

During the ten-second rewind, I grabbed Darcy's brush from her purse and scanned the restroom. All I could find was a small tube of toothpaste. Perfect. I squirted it on the bristles, then stuffed it back into Darcy's purse.

This time, when she grabbed it, she smeared toothpaste through her hair.

The brush dropped as she stared at herself in the mirror. "What. Is. Going. ON!" Her scream echoed through the room, and the clique exchanged stunned glances.

The look in my eyes said it all: Poor Darcy.

Do-Over Day Fourteen

My next opportunity for a Darcy Do-Over came the following day at lunch.

"Hey, girls, watch me in action," Darcy said with a sly grin. She tossed her head toward a table of boys.

"I'm having a much-too-good hair day to waste it without Eric noticing," she said, having bounced back from her unusually *bad* hair day. "I'll go tell him what a great game he pitched."

Jen wrinkled her nose. "Uh, Darcy . . . ," she said, "before you go, you might want to get that gob of broccoli off your front tooth."

Darcy gasped as the other girls giggled.

Perfect.

I rubbed my locket. "Do-over."

"Hey, girls, watch me in action," Darcy repeated. "I'm having a much-too-good hair day to waste it without Eric noticing. I'll go tell him what a great game he pitched."

"Jen, a bug is crawling up your arm!" I yelled.

"Eeewww!" Jen shrieked, jumping up from her chair and swatting at her arms. "Where? Where?"

Darcy had already headed toward Eric's table.

Sweet.

"Where's the bug?" Jen said, still rubbing her arms.

"Oh . . . ," I said. "It must have crawled off."

We watched Darcy flirting with Eric. All I could see was her back, but that was enough. As she twirled a lock of hair, Eric and his friends exchanged sideways glances. Soon their silent communication got the best of them. Eric burst into laughter, burying his reddened face in his chest. His friends guffawed. Darcy looked confused, then turned on her heel and stomped back to our table.

"What are they laughing at?" she growled.

"Uh . . ." Jen pointed at Darcy's mouth.

"What!" Darcy squealed.

"You have broccoli in your teeth," I said matter-of-factly.

Darcy looked horrified. "Omigod!" She dabbed a napkin against her teeth. "Why didn't you tell me?"

We shrugged. "Didn't notice," I said.

Darcy flung her perfectly manicured fingernails into the air. "I'm ruined!"

I subtly raised a single eyebrow. *That's the idea.*

Next Darcy Do-Over:

We were sitting in science class when the fire drill bell rang. Our class walked down the hall to the front door, then out into the parking lot.

Everyone started dispersing into small groups. It had rained the night before, and mud puddles covered the parking lot. This could get interesting. . . .

A few minutes later, a car pulled into the lot. As it drove past us, a tire rolled through a mud puddle and shot a fountain of dirty water into the air. No one was close enough to the puddle to get slimed . . . yet.

I rubbed my locket. "Do-over."

Ten-second rewind.

I slipped away and dropped a piece of paper into the puddle. Then I hurried over to Darcy.

"Hey, Darcy," I said, pointing to the paper. "Isn't that the love poem you were doodling about Eric last period?"

Darcy glanced at the paper and gasped.

She dashed toward the puddle to retrieve the paper. Just

131

as she plucked it out of the puddle, along came the car, spewing her with mud.

"Eeee-*eeewwwww!*" she screamed. Every eye turned toward her. As water dripped from her skin, she stood there soaked and mud-splattered from head to toe. She crushed the soggy paper without looking at it.

Everyone laughed uproariously.

"Darcy, don't you think that shade of brown clashes with your outfit?" someone piped up.

"Did you wash your hair last night?" someone else said. "It looks a little greasy." Obviously, Darcy had shot enough poison barbs to make people enjoy putting her on the receiving end.

"Awesome fire drill!" another voice called out.

Really, no need to thank me, I thought. *Happy to oblige.*

Do-Over Day Fifteen

My next Darcy Do-Over was the following day during social studies class. The teacher had darkened the room as she flashed slides from a projector onto a white screen. We jotted down notes as new images flashed every few seconds. Well . . . most of us jotted down notes. Darcy snoozed with her head on her desk. When the teacher asked me to turn the light on, Jade shook Darcy awake. Darcy sat straight up as if she'd been paying close attention.

What a fake.

I rubbed my locket. "Do-over."

Ten-second rewind. This time, instead of waiting for the teacher to ask me, I flipped the switch as soon as the last slide appeared. The room was flooded with light. The slide show was over, but now everyone was treated to some real entertainment: Darcy snoring with her head on the desk, drooling from the side of her mouth.

"DARCY DIXON!"

Darcy jolted awake and banged her chin on the desk. She grabbed her chin, which caused her to lose her balance and tumble to the floor.

There she sat, sprawled on the floor in a heap.

The class roared in appreciation.

"Ms. Dixon," the teacher said in an icy voice. "I'll be interested in seeing how well you understood the slide show presentation. Please stay after school today for a pop quiz."

Darcy's jaw dropped. Stifled giggles snaked their way through the classroom. Darcy huffed and wiped the drool off her face.

Aww. Poor Darcy.

✪

    LaniAck: What is going on? Tell me about
Project Darcy!

Lani had already logged on to the computer by the time I got home from school.

    DolfinGrl: Let's just say she's had a few
    "incidents." There was broccoli involved. And
    mud. And window cleaner. A long story.
    LaniAck: ELSA! I'm dying of curiosity.
WHAT R U DOING TO DARCY?

DolfinGrl: Nothing more than she deserves. Hey . . . Dad says you can come over the weekend after next. Ask your mom and let me know. GTG. TTYL.

✪

As much fun as my Darcy Do-Overs had been so far, the best was yet to come.

I was headed to my locker when I overheard Darcy talking to Carter at her locker.

". . . I'll just copy off Elsa's paper," Darcy said. "She's so easy to cheat off of. She didn't even defend herself when Mr. Wright accused her of copying. Her copying me! Classic!" She dissolved into giggles.

My mind raced. Did I have time? Yes. Mr. Wright's classroom was just a few feet away.

"Do-over."

Ten-second rewind.

I dashed into Mr. Wright's classroom.

"Mr. Wright!" I said breathlessly. "Can you come with me for just a second?"

I guess I looked panic-stricken enough that Mr. Wright assumed there was an emergency. He didn't ask any questions, just hurried behind me as I dashed back to the corner of the hall, where I could hear Darcy but couldn't see her . . . and vice versa.

"What is it, Elsa?" Mr. Wright asked in alarm.

"Uh . . ."

". . . I'll just copy off Elsa's paper," Darcy was repeating.

"She's so easy to cheat off of. She didn't even defend herself when Mr. Wright accused her of copying. Her copying me! Classic!" She dissolved into giggles.

Mr. Wright still looked a little confused but now was more interested in what he was overhearing.

"I knew she wouldn't," Darcy continued. "Every once in a while, she tries to show sparks of coolness, but she's a goody-goody deep down. I'm thinking my grades are definitely on the upswing with her around. Good thing, too. . . . After my last report card, I almost got kicked off the cheerleading squad."

Mr. Wright cleared his throat and rounded the corner of the hall.

"Darcy," he said, "I'd like to see you in my room. Right now."

EIGHTEEN

ROUGH DRAFT #2

What I've Learned in Seventh Grade
By Elsa Alden

I'll just cut to the chase: What I've learned in seventh grade is that people are horrible.

Pretty harsh, right? Well, it's a pretty harsh world. When we were little, we learned that other people would treat us the way we treated them. We were told that if we were kind and friendly and accepting, other people would return the favor.

Wrong. Just plain wrong. Period.

In seventh grade, I've learned that people are sneaky and selfish. Be nice and get your heart stomped. Wear the wrong clothes and get tortured by the fashion police. Speak up in class or voice an opinion and duck as your classmates shoot daggers from their eyes. Offer to help someone with her homework and watch her stab you in the back. That's what I've learned in seventh grade.

That's why I'm trying to learn new rules. The Golden Rule isn't working for me, that's for sure. Nobody gave me a copy of the new rule book, so I'm feeling my way along. Maybe I'm making a couple of mistakes along the way, but I'm starting to catch on.

This would never fly as a school essay, but it captured the moment.

I hit the Delete key.

✿

I had a hard time getting to sleep that night. I gazed at Mom's picture . . . usually that helped lull me to sleep. But that night, I couldn't look at it.

Mom? I said in my head, looking at the stars on my ceiling. *Am I doing okay? Darcy deserves a little grief, right? I'm just balancing things out.*

Silence.

Then there was a knock on my door. My heart skipped a beat. Was Mom back?

"Come in."

Grandma poked her head in.

"Hi, Grandma," I said. She smiled, walked over and sat beside me.

"Hi, honey," she said. "I had a feeling you were still awake."

I looked into her pretty brown eyes, shaped just like Mom's. "How did you know?"

She shrugged. "Just a feeling. I used to get that kind of feeling sometimes with your mom . . . wondering if something was wrong before she got around to telling me."

I pulled the sheets closer to my chin. "Nothing's wrong, Grandma," I said.

She nodded but was quiet for a long moment.

"Grandma . . . ?" I finally said.

"Yes, honey?"

"If someone was mean to you, and you had a chance to get even . . . not in some evil, horrible way, just in a harmless kind of way . . . would you do it?"

Grandma thought for a minute, smoothing my hair with the palm of her hand. "Well, first of all," she finally said softly, "I'm not sure what you mean by harmless. If you're acting on revenge, there's a pretty good chance that someone's getting hurt."

"Not revenge," I clarified. "Justice."

Grandma nodded. She took my hand in hers and squeezed it gently. "Honey," she said, "adolescence is a difficult time under the best of circumstances, and your circumstances are pretty close to the worst. You've started a new school in the middle of seventh grade and you don't have your mom." She stared at me intently. "But you do have me. If someone is giving you a hard time, maybe I can help."

"I think I'm doing okay," I said hesitantly. "It just seems like everybody's so . . . fake. You know?"

Grandma squeezed my hand tighter. "Honey, at your age, everyone is trying out different personalities and figuring out what works best for them." She shrugged. "Some are clumsier at it than others. But that doesn't mean they're bad people. It just means they're still learning." She grinned. "Believe it or not, as wondrously brilliant and mature as you are, you're still learning, too. That's part of what growing up is all about."

I wasn't entirely convinced.

"But still," I persisted, "sometimes wrong is just wrong, no matter how old you are."

Grandma nodded. "Right you are," she said. "And when someone does something wrong, you should stand up for what's right." She winked. "Your mom was really good at that. But, sweetie, the old cliché is true: Two wrongs don't make a right. You have to be true to yourself."

Be true to yourself, Elsa. That's all I ask.

I shuddered as if a cold breeze had just blown over me. Was that Mom's voice I'd heard? Maybe Mom's voice and Grandma's voice were kind of . . . the same. After all, Mom was the mother she was because of the kind of mother Grandma had been to her. I sat up and hugged Grandma very, very tightly.

"I love you," I whispered in her ear as she hugged me back.

Mom was still watching over me . . . just blending in. And in the meantime, Grandma was right here. In my arms. For the first time in a long time, I suddenly felt very lucky.

NINETEEN

Do-Over Day Seventeen

"This has been positively, absolutely the worst week of my entire life!"

Darcy didn't bother to say hello when I answered the phone Saturday morning.

"Darcy . . . ?" I asked innocently.

"Yes, Darcy!" she spat. "I don't understand why my life is turning into a disaster! I've made a fool of myself a million times over and I got totally busted for copying your paper. . . ." Her voice trailed off in despair.

A smile crept over my face. "It's not so bad," I said in a syrupy-sweet voice. "It's just one little homework grade. No biggie, right?"

She huffed in frustration. "It's a biggie to me!" she said. "If I get another D on my report card, I won't be able to cheer next year!"

Oh, horrors. How would mankind survive? I yawned. "I'm sure your mom will let you cheer next year," I said.

"My mom?" Darcy sniffed. "My mom couldn't care less what I do. It's the school that won't let me cheer without at least a B-minus average." She paused. "I need your help, Elsa."

"My help?"

"Yes. That stupid book we're reading in language arts . . . gag! It's so boring, I can't concentrate on a single sentence. Give me some notes or . . . or something!"

I rolled my eyes. "I'm busy working on your essay, remember?"

"The essay!" Darcy's voice brightened. "Of course. Elsa, I really need that laptop, and the extra credit for the essay might save my grade. You've got to make it really good!"

I paused long enough to make her nervous.

"Elsa!" she barked. "You promised you'd help me! I helped you with your makeup."

I gritted my teeth. *Okay, Darcy, you asked for it.* "I'll help you," I finally said. *Oh, I'll help you, all right.*

True, two wrongs didn't make a right. But Darcy was so . . . so . . . nervy, it made me want to scream. I'd already decided after my talk with Grandma that I'd played my last mean trick on her. Mean tricks were wrong, and Darcy was bound to catch on that whenever something awful happened to her, I was close by. Still, if she was irresponsible enough to let me write her essay, she deserved whatever kind of essay she got . . . right? True, she and her clique would never speak to me again, but at this point, that suited me fine.

"I'll write your essay for you," I said. If I was going to end a friendship, I'd end it with a bang.

Darcy sighed with relief. "Get started this minute! It has to be really good. Remember, it's due a week from Monday."

"I have to write mine, too," I said. "I can't give it to you until right before it's due."

"I've got an idea," Darcy said. "The winner gets to read the essay in front of the whole school on Honors Day. I'll need practice reading it out loud. Have it ready by next Saturday night. I'm having some friends over and I'll read it then."

"A party? Were you planning on inviting me?"

"Well, duh. I'm inviting you now. Besides, a party is the least I deserve after the kind of week I've had."

"Don't you need to ask your mom first?"

"I told you, my mom doesn't care what I do," she said in a haughty voice. "She won't even be here."

"Your mom lets you have a party without her there?"

"Duh," Darcy said. "She's too busy with her new boyfriend to notice if the house gets trashed." She paused, then resumed her orders: "So work on it this week and bring it Saturday night. Got it?"

"Yeah," I said. *I got it.*

TWENTY

Do-Over Day Twenty-two

"Do you believe in ghosts?"

Martin probably wasn't expecting a heavy conversation as he pulled weeds out of my grandmother's garden the next Thursday afternoon, but when I brought him a glass of lemonade, it seemed like the most natural thing in the world to ask.

Martin looked up, rubbing the back of his hand across his forehead and leaving a dirty smear.

"What?" he said.

"Ghosts. Do you believe in ghosts?"

Martin sat on the ground and drank his lemonade. I sat beside him.

"I'm not talking about spooks who wear white sheets and say 'boo,' " I said. "Just . . . people. People who have died but find a way to connect with us."

Martin shrugged. "Who knows what happens after we die? It's the great unknown."

I picked up a dandelion and tapped its tufts with my fingertip. "What if it's not?" I asked.

Martin looked curious. "What do you mean?"

"Well . . . psychics say they can communicate with dead people."

He laughed. "You've noticed that no psychic has ever won the lottery."

"Meaning what?"

"Meaning psychics are scam artists."

I swallowed hard, still unsure how far I intended to go. "Unless it really is possible to communicate with the dead."

Martin shook his head, trying to follow. "What are you talking about?"

Suddenly, I felt like a volcano a century overdue for eruption. Could I trust Martin with this information? Something told me I could. "My mom's dead," I finally said. "An aneurysm. She died last year."

Martin blushed, looking uncomfortable. "Right . . . ," he mumbled with downcast eyes.

"Martin, listen. She died last year, but I saw her a few weeks ago."

Martin bit his bottom lip, trying somehow to piece this loopy conversation together. "Ummm . . . where? Like in a dream?"

I shook my head. "No. I was wide awake in my bed, and suddenly she was by my side. I could see her, touch her . . . I could smell her, Martin." I sighed. "She smelled like lavender, just like when she was alive."

I looked at him nervously. I was prepared for a do-over, but he nodded. "I've read that stress can make the mind play tricks on itself," he responded evenly.

I rolled my eyes. "It wasn't my imagination, Martin. My mom really came to me." I paused, searching his eyes. "She said she's always watching over me, but she's usually blending in, like the stars and the moon blend into the sky during the day. But she got special permission to make an actual visit." Suddenly, making him believe me seemed like the most important thing in the world. "Martin—my dead mother came to see me."

"You're joking with me . . . right?"

I slowly shook my head.

A flash of anger crossed his face. "Do you think I'm an idiot?"

"No," I said earnestly. "I think you're the smartest person I know, which is why I'm telling you. I thought you could help me understand it."

"Understand what?" he said, still wary. "That your mom is a ghost? Or that you're putting me on so you and your snob friends will have something to snicker about over lunch?"

I sighed. Was that what he thought of me? Of course it was.

Grandma's words floated into my head: *"Believe it or not, as wondrously brilliant and mature as you are, you're still learning, too."*

I felt ashamed of myself. I had to make things right. I had to make Martin believe me.

"Martin, listen to me," I said. "When Mom came to see

me, I didn't believe it, either. I woke up the next morning and thought it was a dream. Until . . ."

Martin still looked angry, but now he looked curious, too. "Until what?"

I tilted my chin upward, staring him squarely in the eyes. "Until I had proof."

Martin's eyes squinted. "Proof," he repeated.

I nodded. "Proof. You see, before Mom went back to . . . I don't know, heaven, or wherever . . . she left me with . . . with kind of a gift."

"Like a set of Tupperware on your dresser?"

I shook my head impatiently. "No. A gift proving that maybe there are more dimensions in the world than we realize. Maybe things are happening around us that we can't see or understand."

Martin nodded. "You're making fun of my interest in existentialism," he concluded glumly.

"Your what? Martin, NO!" I yelled. "Quit second-guessing me and listen."

He sighed. "I'm listening. What was your gift?"

A soft spring breeze blew across our faces. "The gift of time . . . the one thing I didn't get enough of with my mom." I leaned in closer to him. "She gave me the ability to turn back time."

Martin massaged his temples with his fingertips. "You're losing me, Elsa," he said wearily.

"Stick with me. She made it possible for me to turn back time ten seconds . . . just long enough to rewind a stupid joke, or undo a slip on a banana peel."

Martin was staring at me like I had grown an extra head. (Now, *that* I can't pull off.)

"Did you notice all the weird, embarrassing things that happened to Darcy last week?" I continued.

A glimmer of recognition flashed in his eyes. "It did seem weird that she kept making a fool of herself. It was almost like some bizarre cosmic balancing act."

"It was. Only I was pulling the strings. When I first had my do-over power . . . that's what Mom calls it . . . I used it to try to make myself popular. Then I saw I could use it to make Darcy unpopular when I realized what a snobby fake she was."

"By turning back time . . . ," he said slowly.

"Only ten seconds. And I won't have this power forever. Just until my thirteenth birthday on May eleventh . . . ten days from now."

The breeze blew a lock of hair into Martin's eyes. He hastily brushed it aside. "Can I get back to my weeds now?"

I threw my hands up. How could I have expected him to believe this incredible story? Then a thought flashed into my mind.

"I'll prove it."

"Proof's a good concept," Martin said.

"Right. Just give me a second."

I glanced around Grandma's yard. There were some squirrels scampering around, and a butterfly or two flitting through the air, nothing out of the ordinary. Hmmmm. . . .

Grandma opened the kitchen window and tossed some

coffee grounds into the yard. "Makes good mulch, I hear," she said.

Perfect. Thanks, Grandma.

I rubbed my locket. "Do-over."

Ten-second rewind.

"Martin, listen closely," I said quickly. "Grandma's about to open the kitchen window, throw coffee grounds into the yard and say, 'Makes good mulch, I hear.' "

"What?" Martin said. "You really are certifiable."

Grandma opened the kitchen window, tossed some coffee grounds out and said, "Makes good mulch, I hear."

Martin looked stunned, then shook his head. "You planned that," he said.

"I didn't plan it, Martin. I lived it. I saw Grandma do that; then I rubbed this magic locket Mom gave me and said 'Do-over' and the world rewound ten seconds. That's how I could tell you exactly what would happen."

His weird expression said he wasn't buying it.

Then I heard a crash next door. Our neighbor had been carrying her metal trash can and had accidentally dropped it onto the patio. She quickly righted it, but it was another chance to convince Martin that I wasn't nuts.

I rubbed my locket. "Do-over."

Ten-second rewind.

"Martin," I said, "our neighbor is carrying her trash can to the patio. In about five seconds, she's going to accidentally drop it and—"

Crash!

Martin jumped so abruptly that I burst into laughter. His jaw dropped as he gazed at me with widened eyes.

"Elsa . . . you're freaking me out! How did you know?"

I laughed out loud. "I told you I was telling the truth."

Martin held his head in his hands, trying to sort through what he'd just witnessed. "There has to be a logical explanation . . . ," he muttered.

"Does there? Why does everything have to be logical?" I asked.

Martin rolled his eyes. "Because there are certain rules about time, motion, physics . . ." He paused while he thought. "Your grandmother and neighbor could have been in on the joke."

Now it was my turn to roll my eyes. "That's a lot of trouble to go to for a joke," I said reasonably. "And our timing would have to be impeccable."

"Still, it makes more sense than . . . than rubbing a necklace and rewinding the world for ten seconds."

Grandma's cat, Snowball, scampered into the yard and plopped into my lap.

Martin inhaled and held a finger under his nose. "Ah . . . ah . . . ah-choo!"

Then he sneezed a second, third and fourth time.

Perfect.

I rubbed my locket. "Do-over."

Ten-second rewind. "Okay, Martin," I said quickly, "Snowball is about to jump into my lap. You're going to sneeze four times in a row."

Before he could respond, out came Snowball, jumping into my lap. Martin looked like he was trying to resist the urge to sneeze, but he couldn't do it. He sneezed once . . . twice . . . three times . . . four times.

"There," I said, feeling satisfied. "I can't plan your sneezes, can I?"

Martin tossed his head backward. "Unbelievable . . . ," he said. "Bogus. Totally bogus." He was talking more to himself than to me. Then he peered at me curiously. "So you really set Darcy's disasters in motion?"

"Guilty as charged." I shrugged and stared at my hands. "It seemed like a good idea at the time."

Martin bounced with a sudden rush of excitement. "It was a brilliant idea!" he exclaimed. "And we still have another week to go!" He flung his hands into the air. "Do you realize what this means? We can make things right! We can change everything!"

I shook my head. "I've made plenty of mistakes," I said, "but there's one thing I've learned for sure: You really can't change anyone except yourself."

Where had I heard that before?

"What are you saying?" Martin said. "You've got this awesome power, and you're not going to do anything with it?"

The spring breeze felt light and crisp against my skin. "The truth is, except for the fun of giving Darcy some payback, I've been less satisfied with my do-overs than with how things happened the first time around."

"But your mom gave you this power for a reason," Martin persisted.

"Exactly. I think I'm finally understanding what that reason was." I smiled. "Look, Martin, if an asteroid suddenly crashes on your head, I won't hesitate to rewind the world and push you out of the way. Otherwise, I think I'll just live my life and trust that I'll be able to handle whatever comes my way . . . the first time around."

"But Darcy's disasters," he said, his voice full of disappointment. "They were classic. For those glorious few days, it seemed like life was balancing out a little bit."

"Well," I said, standing up and brushing the grass off my legs, "it just so happens that I have one more surprise in store for Darcy. But I don't need my do-over power to pull it off."

Martin looked intrigued. "What is it?"

"Darcy's having a party at her house Saturday night. My best friend, Lani, is spending the weekend, so we'll go together. Be at my house by seven and come with us." I grinned, pushing a lock of hair behind my ear. "You won't regret it."

TWENTY-ONE

What I've Learned in Seventh Grade
By Darcy Dixon

What I've learned in seventh grade is that nobody matters but me. You see, in the warped world of middle school, I have real power. I have beauty. I have charm. I couldn't care less about other people's feelings. This, I've learned, is the perfect combination for achieving popularity, and that's all that matters to me.

True, popularity kind of fell into my lap . . . I didn't ask to be beautiful, after all . . . but now that I realize its power, I'll do anything to hold on to it. This often involves squashing other people's feelings or making them feel so awful about themselves that they can't possibly nudge me aside as the most popular girl in seventh grade. I trick people into thinking they are my friends, but I am far superior to them.

This takes energy, of course . . . energy that I could spend doing things that really matter, like finding ways to help others or actually studying for a test . . . maybe even completing a homework assignment without copying somebody else's . . . but those things require effort. They require values. They require caring about the difference between right and wrong. They require me to have at least a single shred of interest in other people.

And I don't. The only person I care about is me. I've learned that middle school actually rewards my value system. I love middle school because middle school loves me. It's a complicated chain of love that only I understand. Some people think that middle school is about getting an education. Little do those crazy people know. It's about being popular. It's about me. And that, I've learned, is all that matters.

Do-Over Day Twenty-three

"Have you finished my essay yet?"

Darcy rushed to my locker the next morning as I grabbed my language arts book.

"Well?" she demanded. "Have you?"

I smiled sweetly. "Just putting a few finishing touches on it," I said. "I want it to be perfect, after all."

Darcy sighed with relief. "Good. It must be perfect, Elsa. That extra-credit grade is the only thing that will keep me from getting thrown off the cheerleading squad." She gave me a serious look. "I'm counting on you." She smiled, tilting her head to one side. "That's what best friends are for . . . right?"

I smiled back. "Don't worry; I'll bring the essay to your party tomorrow night. You can read it there, just like we planned."

She nodded.

"Oh, Darcy, you don't mind if I bring a couple of friends with me, do you?"

She looked suspicious.

"Friends?"

"Yeah . . . just a couple."

"Well . . . don't bring any dweebs over."

I crinkled my nose. "As if."

Do-Over Day Twenty-four

Lani's mom hadn't even turned off the ignition before Lani jumped out of their car and onto Grandma's driveway.

"Elsa!"

"Lani!"

We bounced up and down as we hugged. I hadn't seen her since I'd moved more than a month before, and I hadn't realized how much I missed her. Lani. A real friend who really knew me and liked me just the way I was. I'd never appreciated that as much as I did right then.

She grabbed her overnight bag. As Grandma came

outside to say hello and invite Lani's mother in for a glass of iced tea, Lani and I dashed to my room. Giggling gleefully, we plopped onto the bed and gazed up at my plastic stars.

"Tell me everything," Lani cooed. "What did you do to Darcy? And if you tell me you can't tell me, I'll scream."

"I can't tell you."

Lani screamed, and I giggled.

"What is going on with you, Elsa? You used to tell me everything!"

"Well, my life has gotten a lot more complicated lately," I explained, which was the ultimate understatement. "I can't give you any details, but I've played a few tricks on Darcy. But you know what? As snotty as she is, the tricks weren't nearly as fun as I thought they'd be."

"No way!" Lani said. "I'd love to knock the Slice Girls down a peg or two if I got the chance."

I shrugged. "I don't like being mean."

"But she was awful to you, right?" Lani persisted.

"Yeah. . . ." I gave her a sideways glance and grinned. "Well, okay, I'll admit: It was a little fun. But only a little. And . . ."

Lani leaned in closer.

"Actually . . . ," I said, sitting up, "I have one bit of unfinished business to take care of."

"What?"

"You'll find out tonight. We're going to a party."

TWENTY-TWO

Martin rang Grandma's doorbell promptly at seven p.m. Lani and I rushed to the door to let him in.

I was startled for a second when I opened the door. Martin looked different somehow . . . same glasses, same braces, but . . . I couldn't put my finger on it. He held his head a little higher, his shoulders a little straighter. He had a new air of confidence about him.

"Hi, Martin," I said, trying to conceal my surprise. "This is my friend Lani."

"Hi," he said, and Lani blushed. As my dad walked in and said hello, Lani pulled me aside. "This is the dweeb?" she whispered. "He's, like, a total hottie!"

Well . . . I wouldn't go that far.

"Okay, guys," Dad said. "I guess I'm your chauffeur."

"Oh, I don't mind driving, Mr. Alden," Lani teased, and Dad winked at her.

"Maybe some other time. But don't worry; I'll wear a bag over my head when I introduce myself to Darcy's parents."

Darcy's parents? Uh-oh.

"Uh, Dad . . . ," I said nervously.

"Yeah, honey?"

"I don't think Darcy's parents will be there. She lives with her mom, and she'll be out tonight."

Dad shook his head. "Sorry, guys. You're not going to an unchaperoned party. Does Darcy's mother know about this party?"

"Yes, Dad!" I said, feeling panicky. "Darcy's mom, like, totally trusts her. It'll be fine."

"Sorry, honey," Dad said.

Yikes!

"Dad," I said, trying to sound calm and reasonable, "how about a compromise? We'll only stay a few minutes." Just long enough to launch my stealth bomb, then run for cover. "Can you take us there and let us hang out for just a few minutes?"

Dad looked suspicious. "A few minutes?"

"We're not really going for the party," I explained. "I just have to drop something off for Darcy. You'll be right there waiting for us. Please, Dad?"

He didn't look totally convinced, but finally he shrugged. "Okay," he said. "I'll be waiting in the driveway."

I kissed his cheek. "No prob."

We headed out the door and piled into the car. Dusk had already fallen, and crickets were chirping. I clutched Darcy's essay in my hand. No one else had seen it. Martin and Lani knew I had something up my sleeve, but the details were my little secret. No point in spoiling the fun.

When we pulled up to Darcy's house, kids were milling around . . . some on the front lawn.

"What is her mother thinking?" Dad muttered.

"Please stay in the car," I said. "Please, Dad. I'll drop this off to Darcy and introduce her to Lani. Fifteen minutes, tops. Okay?"

Dad looked nervous but sighed and said, "Okay."

Lani, Martin and I went to the open front door. We elbowed our way past some people coming out, then stood in Darcy's living room, where more people were hanging out. Darcy spotted us and walked over.

"Elsa," she said, managing a fake smile. She spoke into my ear. "You brought Martin?" she whispered fiercely. "Omigod!"

I cleared my throat nervously. "Right. Martin and my friend Lani. Lani, this is Darcy."

Lani smiled and flashed a quick wave.

"Who's that in the driveway?" Darcy asked, peering out the window.

"My dad," I said apologetically. "He's waiting for us. We can't stay long."

"Whatever. Hand over the essay."

"Can't we have a few chips and some punch first?"

Darcy rolled her eyes. "I think there's a bowl of tortilla chips around here somewhere, but they're kind of stale. Mom isn't big on grocery shopping."

Lani looked confused. "So . . . what do you do for meals?"

Darcy shrugged. "Mom's usually out with her boyfriend. Sometimes she leaves me money for pizza. When I told her last night that I'd eaten cold leftover pizza for the third night in a row, she told me I needed to drop a few pounds anyhow."

Lani looked shocked. "What about your dad?" she asked, as usual blurting out exactly what was on her mind.

Darcy looked puzzled. "What about him?"

Lani shrugged. "Does he cook? Does he take you out?"

Darcy curled her lip. "He doesn't exactly have time to make like Betty Crocker," she said with a snarl. "He lives in L.A., making movies. But one of my mom's boyfriends owns a burger joint, and he lets me eat for free. Every once in a while, he even lets me go wild at the mall with his credit card."

She suddenly seemed annoyed. "Like, why are we talking about my mother's boyfriends?" she said.

"So you're here by yourself when your mom goes out?" Lani persisted.

"Duh," Darcy said. "Do I look like a baby? I think I was seven the last time Mom called a sitter. I can take care of myself." Her cell phone rang. She flipped it open and held it to her ear.

"What, Mom?" she spat when she realized who was calling, then started to back down a hallway. She turned toward a wall and put a finger in her other ear. At first, her voice was hushed, but soon she was shouting.

"No, Mother!" she said angrily. "I went to see Dad two weeks ago. I am not going back on Father's Day. Do you think I enjoy sitting in a waiting room for four hours just so

I can get frisked by a prison guard and spend twenty minutes with my dad?"

Martin, Lani and I exchanged embarrassed glances. Prison? Darcy's dad wasn't a big-time Hollywood movie producer. He was in prison.

Just then, Darcy glanced up and caught my eye. Uh-oh. . . .

Her face turned pale and she snapped her phone shut.

"What did you hear?" she asked in a shaky voice, walking toward me.

"Nothing," I insisted.

Her eyes softened and she looked at me pleadingly. "Don't rat me out, Elsa," she said in barely a whisper.

"Of course I won't," I said, feeling a sudden urge to touch her arm.

Her eyes searched mine; then she abruptly tossed her hair back and tipped her nose skyward. "You're toast if you do," she growled. "Now, where's my essay?"

"Right." The essay. The one about Darcy the phony snob. The one that would finally put her in her place and embarrass her enough to shake up her perfect little world. Except now her world seemed anything but perfect.

"Um, Darcy . . . ," I said, knowing I couldn't go through with it. But before I could finish my sentence, Darcy snatched the essay out of my hand and headed toward the center of the room.

She clapped her hands. "People!" she called out. "Everybody gather around. I've got to practice reading my essay out loud."

I felt a thud in the pit of my stomach.

Lani pulled me aside as Darcy stepped onto a low stool and the crowd gathered around her.

"How sad!" she whispered to me.

"What?" I asked, though I already knew what she meant.

"Darcy's life," Lani said. "It's really sad."

"Yeah," Martin agreed. "I didn't know about her dad."

"I don't think she's awful, Elsa," Lani said. "I think she's lonely. School is probably the only place she gets any attention."

The thud in my stomach grew heavier. "Still," I whispered defensively. "She's a total snob. A total fake. You just don't understand."

But suddenly I felt maybe *I* was the one who didn't understand.

Darcy was clearing her throat.

"Okay, here's my essay," she said, opening the folder with her French-manicured nails. "What I've Learned in Seventh Grade, by Darcy Dixon." She smiled coyly. "That's me."

My great idea seemed like the worst idea in the whole world. Grandma's voice rang in my head: *The old cliché is true: Two wrongs don't make a right.*

Darcy started reading: "What I've learned in seventh grade is that nobody matters but me. You see, in the warped world of middle school, I have real power. I have beauty. I have charm. I couldn't care less about other people's feelings."

I felt Lani's and Martin's eyes boring into me. I spun

around to face them, then realized I couldn't look them in the eye. They looked so disappointed in me.

"Do-over!"

Ten-second rewind.

"Okay, here's my essay," Darcy said, opening the folder. "What I've Learned in Seventh Grade, by Darcy Dixon." She smiled coyly. "That's me."

I ran over and grabbed the folder out of her hand. "Darcy, no!"

Her eyes widened and her jaw dropped. "Elsa! What are you doing?"

I clenched the folder tightly in my hand. "Darcy, I'm sorry," I said, my mind racing as I tried to decide what to say next. "I can't write your essay for you."

She hopped off the stool and put her hand on her hip. "But you promised! The essays are due Monday! My cheerleading!" she wailed.

"Darcy," I reasoned, "I tried to write it . . . really I did. But I don't know what you've learned in seventh grade. I don't know anything about you. I thought I did. . . ."

"Well, we'll just have to fake it then, won't we!" she said through clenched teeth, trying to grab the essay from my fingers.

"No," I said calmly. "I don't want to fake it anymore." I sighed. "Darcy, you can work on your essay all day tomorrow. You can do it. You don't need me to tell you about your own life. The only one who can write your essay is you. Otherwise, we're both fakes, and neither of us deserves that laptop, or the extra-credit grade."

Her eyes narrowed into slits. "Well, aren't you Little

Miss Goody-Goody!" she sputtered. "You can take your essay and you can, well, for starters, you can get out of my house!"

I looked her straight in the eye. "I'm sorry, Darcy," I said. I meant it.

TWENTY-THREE

ROUGH DRAFT #3

What I've Learned in Seventh Grade
By Elsa Alden

In Language Arts this year, we read a novel called *To Kill a Mockingbird*. It's mostly about a couple of kids, but it's also about their dad, who always tries to do the right thing and couldn't care less whether anybody else likes it or not. His name is Atticus Finch. What I've learned in seventh grade is that Atticus Finch wouldn't have fit in very well at Harbin Springs Middle School.

It seems like in middle school, all anybody cares about is what other people think. I learned that when you pay more attention to other people's reactions than you do to your own actions, you make a lot of mistakes.

But it's not that we're all totally selfish. We're just kind of trying to figure out who we really are. That's the nice thing about Atticus. He already knows. When you don't know, life becomes a trial-and-error process that leads to lots of mistakes. Those mistakes—gossiping, putting each other down, hurting feelings, building up our egos and trying to hide our flaws—aren't very flattering, but they aren't really as evil as they seem.

We look selfish and silly and shallow when we're trying to fit in, but what we really feel is small and scared.

I'm not sure if I know myself any better now than I did at the beginning of seventh grade. But I have a better idea of who I want to be. I can't truthfully say that I've stopped caring what other people think about me, but I've gotten better at deciding for myself whether their opinions are valid. I've also learned that having someone disapprove of me isn't the end of the world . . . unless it's someone I respect, in which case it definitely feels like the end of the world.

I wonder what Atticus was like in seventh grade . . . maybe no braver than my classmates and me. Maybe he had to learn how to be brave. Maybe he started learning that in middle school. It's a really good place to practice being brave.

I guess what I learned in seventh grade is that I'm learning, just like Atticus was. I want to be brave. I'm working on it.

I reread what I'd typed. I smiled and clicked Save.

Do-Over Day Twenty-six

Martin was waiting for me at my locker Monday morning.

"So," he said, "now will you tell me what happened Saturday night? Where was the big surprise?"

I grinned. "I told you, I changed my mind. As soon as I attain perfection, I'll turn my attention back to Project Darcy. In the meantime, she'll just have to fend for herself."

Martin shook his head. "Girls are so weird," he muttered. "So no more do-overs?"

I crinkled my brow. "Hmmmm. . . . Maybe I can make a quick exception."

Martin smiled but looked skeptical. "What?" he asked.

"Ya ever kiss a girl?" I asked playfully, then laughed as he blushed a bright shade of red. "That's what I thought." I gazed down the hall. "That girl down there by her locker . . . isn't her name Felicity?"

"Yeah . . . ," Martin said dreamily. "Foxy Felicity."

"Go give her a kiss . . . nothing too mushy . . . just enough to get it over with and know what it's like."

"You. Are. Insane," Martin said.

"I'll do it over, and she'll never know it happened. Go ahead, Martin. My gift to you."

He shifted his weight. "I guess I could. . . . But you promise you'll do it over?"

"I promise. Now, go!"

Martin walked over to Felicity, paused for a moment,

166

then suddenly pressed his lips against hers, just for a nano-second.

Felicity looked too stunned to react as Martin pulled away from her, then rushed back to me. "Do it over!" he said frantically.

I grinned. "Uh . . . changed my mind."

"ELSA!"

"Okay, okay!"

I rubbed my locket and said "Do-over," then watched the whole priceless moment become undone.

"Did I do it?" Martin asked breathlessly after he had re-wound his steps back to me.

"Oh, you did it, all right."

His eyes widened. "Did she slap me in the face?"

"No. Actually, she looked kinda . . . okay about the whole thing, in a weird kind of way."

Martin's face brightened. "Really?" He laughed, then bounced on his toes and said, "Can we do it again? This time, concentrate on my form."

I poked him in the chest. "You're on your own from now on, Romeo," I said. "I'm done trying to choreograph the cosmos."

We laughed as we watched Felicity walk down the hall, clueless that she had just given Martin his first kiss.

"Besides," I continued, "my carriage turns back into a pumpkin on my birthday."

"Are you sure, Elsa?" he asked. "Maybe your mom will let you keep your power, or maybe she'll accidentally forget that she gave it to you, or—"

I held out my hand to stop him. "Thanks, but no

thanks," I said, rubbing my locket. "I think I'm kinda getting the hang of things . . . you know?"

"Poor, delusional Elsa," Martin teased. "Don't you know that eighth grade is even worse than seventh? Next year will make this year seem like a piece of cake."

I laughed. "Bring it on. And without supernatural powers, thank you very much." My eyes brightened. "Hey, Martin, we both love to argue. Let's join the debate club!"

"And the National Association of Nerds!" Martin chimed in playfully.

I punched his arm. "At least we'll be in good company."

✿

Martin and I were walking down the hall toward Mr. Wright's room when Carter came up to me.

"Hi, Elsa," she said, pulling me aside and lowering her voice. "I didn't get a chance to say hi to you at Darcy's party."

"That's okay," I said. "I didn't stay long."

Carter looked at her feet, as if trying to decide what to say next. "When Darcy was on the phone talking to her mom . . . ," she finally said, ". . . I heard that, too."

"You mean . . . ?"

Carter nodded. "I had heard rumors about her dad being in jail, but I never believed them. She always had so many stories about visiting him in Hollywood. Now I wonder if anything Darcy says is true."

"Yeah, well . . . I can see how she'd be tempted to stretch

the truth about something like that," I said. "I feel really bad for her."

"Me too, but . . ." Carter's voice trailed off. "I wonder how good a friend Darcy really is. She makes me feel so bad about myself sometimes, you know?"

I knew.

"When I heard her talk about her dad being in jail," Carter said, "I wanted to tell everybody at the party, to get back at her. But you didn't say anything."

I blushed. "I've done some things I'm not very proud of," I said quietly.

"Well, I think you're a good friend." Carter smiled at me.

I smiled back. "Let's just say I'm getting better."

Do-Over Day Thirty

Ow!

My pumps were killing me. At least I was sitting down, for now. And squished toes were a small price to pay to make Grandma happy. She'd asked me to wear a nice dress for Honors Day, which was the least I could do. As our class had filed into the auditorium, with the music teacher banging out our school song on the piano, I'd scanned the audience to find Dad and Grandma. Front row. Naturally.

The principal had already called out all the honors and awards, except one. My skin tingled with excitement. True, it would be pretty excruciating to stand up in front of all these people and read my essay, especially in these pumps . . . but a laptop . . .

"The final award," said the principal, "is for our annual essay contest."

Darcy was glaring at me from a few seats over. I sank a little lower in my chair.

"This year's theme is 'What I've Learned in Seventh Grade,' " the principal continued. "Ladies and gentlemen, I tell you in all sincerity that this year's contest was one of the most difficult to judge. Several of the entries were exceptional. Naturally, there can be only one winner."

In my excitement, I accidentally kicked Martin with a pointy-toed pump.

"Ow," he said.

"My bad."

"And the winner of this year's essay contest is . . ."

I dug my fingernails into the palms of my hands.

". . . Martin King!"

Martin King?

Martin King!

I did a double take. "Martin!" I squealed. "You won!" I felt almost as excited as if I'd won myself. Almost. (A new laptop . . . sigh.)

Martin walked to the microphone to accept a plaque. His essay was waiting on the podium.

"Martin, please read your essay," the principal said.

Martin adjusted his tie and cleared his throat, looking nervous.

He leaned close to the microphone. "What I've—" he began, but he backed off when squeaky feedback blasted from the speakers.

"What I've Learned in Seventh Grade," he began again.

"I started seventh grade thinking I was smarter than everybody else, maybe even the teachers," he read with a slight tremble in his voice. "I thought my intelligence was the most important thing about me, maybe even the only thing that really mattered.

"It was easy to feel better than my classmates, most of whom were more worried about their hairstyles than their grades." His voice sounded stronger, more confident now.

"I didn't think I had anything in common with any of them. I was superior."

Martin paused and his voice softened. "Except that I wasn't. What I've learned in seventh grade is that I used my intelligence to keep people at a distance. If I concentrated on my intelligence, then I wouldn't have to worry about being too shy to say hi to someone in the hall, or feel too embarrassed that I'm a washout on the baseball team.

"What I've learned in seventh grade is that there's more than one way to be a snob. True, I've never been intentionally mean to anyone or started any rumors, or criticized the way someone was dressed"—I noticed several of my classmates looking down at their hands—"but I found my own ways to be a snob.

"Maybe I really *don't* have much in common with many of my classmates," he continued, glancing in our direction. "Or maybe I do and I just don't know it because I haven't given them the chance.

"One thing I've learned is that as much as I enjoy reading books, sometimes it's time to stop reading somebody else's story and start living my own. I'm going to put a little more effort into making friends . . . and into being a friend." He caught my eye and smiled. I smiled back.

"What I've learned in seventh grade is that there's more than one way to be smart. I'm pretty smart in some ways. I'm an idiot in others." He shrugged. "I'm learning. We all are."

He looked up from his paper and gazed at the audience.

"That's what I've learned in seventh grade."

TWENTY-FOUR

"A toast," Dad said, "to our honor student."

Dad, Grandma and I raised our glasses of iced tea and clinked them together. We were having our celebration lunch at a Mexican restaurant after the Honors Day ceremony.

I wrinkled my nose. "Thanks," I said, "but all I got was one measly certificate for the A-B honor roll."

"Well, that one little certificate suits me just fine," Dad said, tousling my hair. "Actually, it was a relief when the principal backed off from his plan to have you skip eighth grade. The thought of enrolling you in medical school before you turned thirteen was a little overwhelming."

I smiled. "Sorry I'm not brilliant like Mom was."

Dad and Grandma exchanged glances. "Elsa, honey," Grandma said softly, "your mom was brilliant in my eyes, but she was just a normal girl at your age."

I shook my head. "No," I said firmly. "Mom was lots of things, but normal wasn't one of them." I got a dreamy look in my eyes. "Mom was perfect."

Dad propped his elbows on the table and leaned his chin on his folded hands. "Honey, it's easy to idealize people after they've died," he said gently, "but I think the best way we can honor Mom's memory is to remember her the way she really was: perfect to us, but with her fair share of flaws, just like everybody else."

I stared at my tea. "I don't remember any flaws."

Dad smiled. "You don't remember how klutzy she was? Like the time she spilled a gallon of paint all over the kitchen floor? Or the time she pulled up too close to the drive-through menu and flattened it like a pancake? And she was always running late."

Grandma chuckled. "Always. And always asking me if I knew where her shoes were. She could never find her shoes!"

My eyes were suddenly moist, but my heart felt light. "Just like me. When I was little, I was scared of monsters hiding under my bed, but Mom said a monster would never be able to fit with all the shoes I had stuffed underneath," I said, laughing softly.

"Thank heaven she kept a pair of flip-flops on the garage steps for emergencies," Dad said. "I think she ended up wearing those flip-flops to my office Christmas party one year."

The ice clinked in our glasses as we laughed and sipped our tea.

I wrinkled my nose and smiled. "I wonder if she ever gossiped," I said.

"I know she did!" Grandma replied cheerfully. "Once, when she was around your age, she got mad at her friend Cara and told everybody that she had six toes. In all!"

I giggled and bit into a tortilla chip.

After our laughter had died down, Grandma swallowed a sip of tea. "But your mother's kindness always won out in the end," she said. "She felt so bad about the six-toes rumor that she bought Cara three new pairs of sandals so everyone would know it wasn't true."

"Why didn't she just lend Cara her emergency flip-flops?" Dad said, and we laughed some more.

Bright piñatas swayed ever so slightly throughout the restaurant, as if a light breeze had just buoyed them from below. My heart felt buoyed, too. I winked into the air, knowing that Mom was blending in.

"Hi, Mom," I whispered to myself. "Thanks for watching out for me."

TWENTY-FIVE

"Yerrrrr out!"

The umpire stuck out his thumb, and the Harbin Springs Middle School batter dropped his bat and trotted to the dugout.

No big deal. Our team was winning by six runs in the top of the ninth inning, so the game was basically in the bag. Even so, I was nervous. As I sat in the bleachers with a baseball cap shielding my face from the late-afternoon sun, all I could think about was Martin. He'd sat on the bench the whole game, just like every other game of the season. He insisted that he didn't care . . . really, he was glad not to make a fool of himself, he assured me . . . but this was the last game of the season, and it wasn't fair that Martin had never even had a chance to bat. He'd had such a great day, winning the essay contest. He had to bat at least once today. I didn't care who won the game; I just wanted to see him play.

Fat chance. With two outs in the ninth inning, the Harbin Springs Middle School baseball team was minutes from wrapping up the season.

"Next up: Martin King."

Martin King? The announcer's voice boomed his name over the loudspeaker. I couldn't believe it. The coach was going to let Martin bat!

"Go, Martin!" I shouted from the stands, jumping to my feet and clapping.

"Who's that kid?" I heard a voice behind me ask.

"Some benchwarmer," came the response. "The coach must figure he can't lose at this point."

Their remarks made me shout even louder. "Knock it out of the park, Martin!" I called, sticking my pinkies into the corners of my mouth and whistling for good measure.

Martin's trip from the dugout to home plate seemed to last an hour. He kept glancing back at the dugout, like he was making sure the coach hadn't made a mistake. The coach waved him on, but Martin looked like he wished the field would swallow him whole.

"You can do it, Martin!" I shouted. *One way or another, you can do it.*

The bat seemed to wobble as he hoisted it behind his shoulder.

"Choke up, kid!" the loudmouth from behind me yelled. Martin's knuckles were white from his death grip on the bat.

"You're doing great, Martin!" I called.

The pitcher threw the ball, but Martin didn't move.

"Stirrr-ike one!" the umpire said.

The pitcher threw a second ball, and again, Martin didn't move.

"Ball!" the umpire said.

Whew.

Then a third ball. Martin stood as still as a statue.

"Stirrr-ike two!"

I bit the fingernails of one hand while I dug the other set into my thigh. *Come on, Martin!*

The fourth ball whizzed by, and Martin didn't move a muscle.

"Stirrr-ike three! Yerrrr out!"

Omigod. . . .

I rubbed my locket. "Do-over!"

The last ten seconds of the game rewound . . . pretty cool watching a ball whiz back to the pitcher . . . and the umpire repeated, "Stirrr-ike two!"

"Martin, swing!" I shouted from the bleachers. "Choke up and swing! I'll get you through this!"

He turned slightly and caught my eye for a second. I smiled and he smiled back. He knew what I meant.

This time, when the ball sailed toward him, Martin swung with all his might . . . and missed. But at least he swung.

I rubbed my locket. "Do-over!"

Ten-second rewind. "I'll get you through this!" I repeated, and he smiled at me.

The pitcher threw the ball, and again, Martin swung as hard as he could.

And missed.

I rolled my eyes. Nothing was easy with Martin. "Do-over."

Ten-second rewind.

"I'll get you through this!"

Martin let the bat fall by his side for a moment while he shook his shoulders to relax. When he hoisted the bat again, his body language was different. He seemed . . . confident.

I whistled again, bouncing in the stands with excitement.

The pitcher threw the ball. Not a great pitch . . . it veered far enough to the right of the bat that the umpire would probably call it a strike . . . except that Martin hit it.

Slammed it, even. Leaning to the right to follow the arc of the ball, Martin dipped into the swing, then leaned into his right knee and smacked the ball so hard that the crack of the bat made me jump.

And I wasn't the only one. As the ball soared high over the pitcher's head and arced toward the outfield, every person in the bleachers was suddenly on his feet. There was a second of stunned silence, then a low appreciative whistle from the bigmouth behind me. (I was starting to like that guy.)

Martin didn't move at first . . . just stood there with his jaw dropped, like the rest of us . . . but as the outfielders lifted their gloves and followed the ball's path, he dropped the bat and started running. As he rounded first base, the ball sailed out of the center fielder's reach and plunked to the ground. The crowd screamed more loudly. Martin rounded second and was headed for third by the time the center fielder caught up to the ball and threw it to second base. The second baseman spun it off to the third baseman . . . who dropped it.

The coach was frantically waving Martin home. With his arms pumping, Martin ran until he was a few feet from the base, then slid into home.

"Safe!"

A home run! The crowd roared.

Martin's teammates rushed from the dugout to slap him on the back as he pumped his arms in the air victoriously. Martin King, cocky? I guess anything was possible.

Our eyes locked as he walked back to the dugout, and I gave him a thumbs-up. The look in his eyes said it all: *Thanks, Elsa.*

But I hadn't hit the ball. He had. He just needed to believe he could do it.

Now he did.

TWENTY-SIX

Do-Over Day Thirty-one

"Hi, sweetie."

I gasped. My eyelids had been fluttering as I drifted on the verge of sleep, but now I was wide awake. Mom was back.

"Mom!" I turned in my bed to face her, then buried my face in her lavender-scented nightgown. "You came back!"

"Well, I couldn't exactly let you turn thirteen without wishing you a happy birthday, now, could I?"

I laughed and cried at the same time. "I want one of your vanilla pound cakes with green frosting," I said. "I refuse to have a birthday without my green birthday cake." I pouted.

Mom winked at me. "I don't think you'll have to," she said. "I was in the kitchen blending in while you were out today, and Grandma was up to her elbows in flour. She might just have a surprise for you in the morning."

I smiled. "It won't be the same."

Mom sighed in mock exasperation. "Come on, now!" she said. "Who do you think taught me how to bake?"

Good point.

I peered into Mom's eyes. "I'm sorry I screwed up, Mom," I said sleepily. "I know I've made a lot of mistakes the past few weeks. If only I'd listened to your advice to be true to myself."

"You were true to yourself, honey," she said, laying her cool palm on my cheek. "Sure, you took a couple of spills along the way, but you found your footing. I knew you would. I'm proud of you."

The tips of Mom's hair brushed against my face. "So," I said, "I guess my powers end at midnight."

"Officially at four twenty-six a.m.," she corrected me. "That's what time you were born." Her eyes sparkled even in the dark. "Do you think you're ready to make it on your own now, minus the do-overs?"

I nodded. "The funny thing is that I think I was ready before. I just didn't know I was." Sometimes perfectly horrible is perfectly fine and you don't know it yet.

She ran her fingers through my hair. "You really are learning!"

I smiled. "Should I give you back the locket?" I asked.

Mom looked like she was thinking it over. "Nah," she finally said. "After tonight, it'll just be . . . well, frankly, a pretty tacky piece of jewelry. So wear it as much as you want. Just don't blame me for turning you into a fashion disaster."

"It's funny," I said, rubbing the locket. "Grandma never came right out and told me, but it seemed like she knew something was up."

Mom nodded. "She's the one who gave the locket to me, you know. I think she had her own experience with it. I don't think it packed quite the punch for either of us that it did for you, but there's definitely something special about it. And it seems to keep getting passed down from one generation to the next . . . which means when your daughter's thirteenth birthday gets close . . . watch out!"

We laughed, but my heart was feeling heavy. I gazed at Mom's face. "Will you come back again, after tonight?"

Mom shrugged. "I'm such a pain that they keep making exceptions for me," she said, making me laugh. "So who knows? Maybe I'll be back."

"Are you scared, Mom? Is it really weird where you are?"

"Nah. Don't be scared of death, baby," she said softly. "It's a piece of cake . . . no pun intended."

I smiled.

"And," she continued, "don't be scared of life. Give it all you've got, kiddo."

I took a long, deep sniff of her skin. "I miss you, Mom. I love you."

"I love you more. One day, you'll know how much, when you have your own daughter."

"No," I said, "I already know."

I gave her a kiss, and she disappeared.

Well . . . blended in.

About the Author

Christine Hurley Deriso began her career in newspaper journalism and has written for numerous national magazines. She is the publications editor at the Medical College of Georgia. Her first book, *Dreams to Grow On,* received the 2003 Independent Publisher Book Award in the category "Most Inspirational to Youth." She and her husband, Graham, live with their children, Gregory and Julianne, in North Augusta, South Carolina.